Tim Lebbon was born in London in 1969. He now lives in Goytre, Monmouthshire, with his wife Tracey. Over the past five years he has had over forty stories published in small press and semi-professional magazines. He has stories upcoming in several anthologies, and is working on a new novel. This is his first book.

MESMER

TIM LEBBON

ISBN 1 901530 02 7

Printed and bound in Great Britain by
Redwood Books, Trowbridge, Wiltshire

British Library Cataloguing in Publication Data.
A catalogue record for this book is available
from the British Library.

Tanjen Ltd
52 Denman Lane
Huncote
Leicester
LE9 3BS

to *Tracey*,
for her patience and support

and

to *Mum & Dad*,
for the way they put my hat on

one

In service stations across the land, the dead walk.

Service stations, the perfect home for the zombie. Neither inviting, nor welcoming. The place where friendly smiles can so easily be lost amid distant stares from strangers and the tired, unseeing gaze of the perpetual travellers, and where day and night are distinguished only by the opening times of the shops. The travellers are always there, whether they move through necessity, desire or frustration. At night the shops are closed but still the toilets are full; if the gambling machines were not locked during the evening, the impersonal beeps and clunks would provide continuous background music to the never ending play of life, and death.

It was at one of these places — the M5 service station at Gordano; humid, warm, the RAC man hot and miserable — that Rick saw his ex-girlfriend.

He was there with Liz, his wife, on the last day of their Easter break, returning from a long weekend in Cornwall. She had just handed him a chocolate flapjack and he still had the brown stain melting on his teeth when he happened to glance across from the shop to the telephones.

And there she was.

His ex had died eight years previously, kidnapped and murdered and left to rot in a foul ditch in Newport. He had gone to her funeral, emotionally paralysed with anger so intense that his teeth worked loose with the strain. Her parents had requested a happy wake with no tears, a celebration of her life rather than a mourning of her death. He had smiled with people he hardly knew and accepted their kind sympathy, and then made his excuses and manoeuvred his way to the bathroom. There he had cried, curled up on the floor next to the bath, noticing that her parents had painted the room for the funeral and smelling her perfume ghosting up from speckled patterns of talc on the carpet. Her mother had found him eventually, held him and cried with him. For a while, minutes that seemed timeless, they had shared grief; she desperate, he uncontrollable. Then they had smiled and hugged and, without speaking, returned to the party. Nobody had mentioned their red eyes.

And there she was.

Pen.

Rick thought she looked ill, but realised the craziness of this: she was dead after all. She was thin and pale and somehow insignificant, people hardly seeming to notice her. She wore black jeans, but where before there had been a delicately rounded behind accentuated by the dark material, now there was only a flat, uninteresting bump. Her hair had changed as well, from dark and luxurious to grey, straggly, unwashed and uninspiring . . .

But she was dead!

'Huh!' Rick grunted. He chewed the flapjack slowly, confusion welling with the shock. Somebody bumped into his shoulder and moved off without apologising. He did not notice.

'Rick?' Liz said. 'What is it?'

The girl he had once loved was talking into the telephone, facing away from him. There was somebody standing behind her waiting to use the 'phone when she had finished, and Rick had to step to one side to get a better view. She half-turned towards him and already he was sure. But no, for God's sake, how could he be sure? How could he stand here and tell himself that he was seeing Pen on the 'phone in these services eight years after he had gone to her funeral and cried into her mother's arms? Stupid, idiotic . . . but it *was* her.

'Rick!' Liz tugged at his elbow. The hand holding the flapjack jerked away from his mouth but he remained staring away from his wife. She shoved him and for a second his eyes wavered towards her, but they were unseeing and distant.

'Rick, people are staring. What's the matter? Come on, let's get back to the car, babe. Rick?'

'Huh?' Rick looked at Liz, smiled at her (and for a moment her hair was black and lustrous, not the blond and short that he had married). 'Sorry?'

'What's wrong? You in a trance, or what? Look where you're going, people will bump into you.'

'Oh, right. Sorry.' Rick looked back to the bank of telephones. She had gone. The person who had been waiting behind her had slipped into the booth and was pumping money into the silver machine. 'Shit!'

'Rick, what the hell . . .?'

'Just going to the loo,' he said quickly. 'That bloody curry last

9

night,' he smiled, but he could see the doubt on Liz's face.

Where the hell had Pen gone?

Rick elbowed his way past a group of football supporters who were loudly announcing the merits of their team above all others. When he turned around Liz was still watching him, frowning. He had reached the 'phones and now had to go to the loo, or else Liz would wonder where he was going, what he was doing. He stepped quickly into the men's toilets, paused just inside the entrance, thinking. An old man with a flat cap and tatty jacket gave him a strange look, probably thinking he was "one of them weirdos or a bloody druggie". Rick hardly noticed, but he became aware that staring off into space in a gents' loo was probably not going to make him very popular.

It was impossible. Pen had died, he had seen her coffin, he had been interviewed by the police and had the press asking ridiculous questions like "how do you feel" and "what do you think of the person who did this?" He had been with her parents when the police had come to the house to inform them that they had found Pen. There had been two detectives, one tall, one short. The tall one had stood at a distance, silent, respectful, while the short one moved slowly into the living room. He had tried not to meet Rick's gaze. He stared at the carpet, at Rick's chest, out of the window, looked at the pictures on the wall. Even before he spoke, Rick was crying, because he knew what the policemen had come to tell them.

Rick had felt an irrational hatred towards this little man who had the insolence to tell them that they had found his girlfriend; dead, half naked, mutilated in a ditch close to a school. Her body had been there for several days, the smell eventually alerting a group of children and teachers to its presence. As Rick was crying, Pen's parents had frowned, shuffled their feet. Her mother had offered the detectives a cup of tea, enquired as to whether they took milk and sugar, asked if they wanted some biscuits. Then she had started to cry, and the detectives had left.

Rick had gone soon afterwards, given a lift home by a friend. His parents had been waiting for him.

Two weeks later, the funeral.

Everyone knew that Pen was dead, that she had been buried eight years ago in a little cemetery in Newport. It had rained, the JCB had stood to one side like a sleeping dinosaur, there had been over a hundred people there. She was dead. Therefore, the person he had seen using the telephone could not have been Pen. End of story, full stop. Except it was her. Rick was sure.

He half turned in the entrance hall to the toilets, letting a couple of football fans breeze past him, fuming alcohol. One of them passed a funny comment, the other laughed and turned to look at Rick. Rick glanced away, at the ceramic tiles on the wall. They were square, patterned in a chequer layout, white and a soft green. Pen had liked green. She had wanted a green kitchen if they ever got around to moving in together.

Rick stepped from the corridor, looking for Liz first. He thought he saw her blond bob in the shop, browsing at the magazines exhorting wealth, health, happiness and multiple orgasms. Feeling guilty, almost as if he was deceiving her, he darted for the exit. A young girl held the door open for him but he was too preoccupied searching for the familiar black hair to remember to thank her.

The parking area was chaotic, and he felt his familiar short

temper coming to the fore as soon as he began dodging the
dawdlers and pushing past the stragglers. It was like a game of
human dodgems, where everyone else was a bad driver. They all
seemed determined to inconvenience Rick as much as possible by
banging his ankles with pushchairs, pausing directly in front of
him to talk to their partners or take a bite out of an ice cream. It
was hot and the sun hats were out in force, shorts concealing pink
thighs and revealing pinker legs to the rays. He felt the prickle of
reawakened sunburn on his shoulders and back.

The smell of exhaust fumes overrode everything else, hanging
in the heavy atmosphere like marsh gas, except more deadly. It
hazed the air, thickened it perceptibly so that a combination of
heat haze and drifting fumes gave the impression of defective eyesight. Anything more than fifty meters away was an indistinct
blur, cars at the other end of the car park little more than coloured
smudges.

He stood outside the doors, standing to one side so that he did
not block the exit and cause a commotion. He turned briefly to
look back into the shop for Liz, but the sun was reflecting from
the glass and blinding him. He could not see in, but she would
surely see out if she decided to look. Still feeling guilty, Rick
stepped further to the side until he was away from the glazed
entrance. He looked out into the car park again, shading his eyes
from the sun, wishing for his sunglasses that were still in the car.
He did a quick sweep of the car park, failed to see any sign of anyone even resembling Pen. He looked again, slower this time, concentrating on individuals rather than simply running his eyes
across the crowd. He saw someone — tall, dark hair — laughing
with a man as they strolled away from the service area. Rick

caught his breath, concentrated on the woman. No. Too tall, hair too dark. The Pen he had seen today had grey streaks in her hair.

Who wouldn't, after having been dead for eight years?

'Oh shit,' Rick sighed. He shrugged his shoulders, grinned to himself in embarrassment. What the hell was he doing? Looking for a dead girlfriend? Yeah, right, well he knew what Liz would have to say about that. She would giggle cruelly and call him an idiot, probably never let him forget it. Like the time he had dreamed that their next door neighbour had passed away, opened the door to her a couple of days later, stood back in terror and kindly informed her that she was dead. Mockery. Well, he could live with it.

For a wistful few seconds he thought back to his time with Pen. He had loved her, a first love that still felt pure and special now. The pain of her death still haunted him and reared its head at the most unexpected, inopportune moments. On the day he had married Liz, he had spent a couple of minutes crying on his best man's shoulder. It had been unavoidable, the thought that he was betraying Pen's memory even though she was no longer with him. But Liz had smiled at this in the special way she seemed to have, stroked his hair, kissed him. Then she said that she hoped Pen would approve of whom he had finally married. That had meant a lot to him then. It still did.

Rick turned and walked back towards the doors. A child stumbled into his legs, and instead of cursing and becoming angry, as he had felt earlier, Rick knelt and helped the little girl back to her feet. Her mother pulled her away, flustered and hot and tired looking. She thanked Rick and left, and it was as Rick watched her hurry towards the shimmering rows of parked cars that he saw

Pen.

She was edging her way between two vehicles, glancing warily around. Her gaze passed over Rick and did not stop.

Rick stood melded to the spot. His heartbeat increased, his breath froze in his lungs, his legs shook, stomach rolled. He could feel his balls tingling with something akin to fear . . . and he realised that, unless Pen had a twin sister who he had not found out about during the two years they spent together, he was looking at Pen now. Pen who was dead. Pen who he had once promised to marry. Pen . . . who was dead.

'Pen?' Rick said. He kept his voice low, as if afraid to verbalise his suspicions. Maybe he was trying to convince himself, trying the name in his mouth again for the first time in years. 'Pen?'

Without looking he stepped into the road, his legs seemingly acting separately to his brain. His sensible self frantically fired angry impulses down neural paths and into the relevant nerves, but his emotions fought them off. Road, road! they hissed, but all his attention was focused on Pen. A car screeched to a halt several steps from him, the driver gesticulating wildly. Luckily it had not been going very fast, but the pained scream of tyres attracted the attention of most of the people around the entrance area.

'Rick!' he heard a voice shout, concerned and confused. Even though his mind identified it as his wife, his body mutinied once more: his imagination overruled the voice and forced him forward again.

He walked towards Pen. She was still there, looking at him strangely, frowning, eyes moving from side to side as if she was trying to spot some small creature that had escaped.

'Pen!' Rick called. 'Pen, it's me, Rick!'

The woman glanced at him. He saw a glimmer of recognition in her eyes, the faintest hint of lost knowledge; it may even have been the heat haze that gave that impression. Then she turned and fled.

Rick almost went after her. Even though he could hear his wife calling him from the other side of the road, even though he knew he was being watched by people who saw him as the token service station oddball, his instincts told him to follow. But by the time he defeated his confusion and his legs began to work, the girl who may have been Pen had reached a large black truck. She climbed into the passenger side and the vehicle pulled away, its exhaust leaving black exclamation marks in the hot summer air. Rick called after it, once, and then came to his senses and tried to see the numberplate. But the truck was too far away. Exhaust fumes foiled his attempt.

There was mixed suspicion and mirth in the eyes of those around him. Some glanced away, embarrassed or nervous. Others continued to watch, unabashed and blatantly accusing him of some unspecified wrongdoing. One of the latter was Liz.

'What was that all about?' she asked.

Rick shrugged. 'Me being daft . . .? The heat . . .? Fuck knows.'

'Ask him, then,' Liz said quietly.

'Who?'

'Fuck.'

'In the car?' he suggested.

Liz glanced at the people who were still watching them and nodded. 'Come on then, silly sod. I've got some apple pies.'

Rick smiled distractedly. 'My favourite.'

'I know,' Liz nodded. 'Now talk.'

Mesmer

*   *   *

Liz sat tight-lipped in the driver's seat, hands at ten to two, eyebrows meeting in a heavy frown. The road ahead was busy and daylight was waning, and she was driving into the sun. The glare inevitably found its way around or through the sun visor.

She was looking forward to crossing the bridge. At least Gwent had road lights, once they approached Newport. And a two lane motorway, she remembered, and traffic jams, and the bloody roadworks for the second Severn crossing that seemed to be taking about three decades to complete. She glanced at the dashboard clock. It was nearly nine, they would be lucky to be home before ten. Tired, irritable, confused . . . mostly confused . . . they would go to sleep angry with each other. Unable to enjoy the closeness they usually felt when they went to bed, the cuddling and the lovemaking that sometimes resulted from it.

Her grandmother had told her never to let darkness drop on bad feelings.

'Shit! Shit . . . shit . . . shit!' she hissed.

Rick glanced across at her, saw her angry expression, decided not to respond to the sudden outburst. Now they were quiet, now the talking was over for the moment, he found himself staring ahead with more than a passing interest in the lorries that drifted by on their left. Liz was motoring, obviously keen to get home. Rick, always comfortable and confident as a passenger but still a little worried at Liz's mood, found himself tense and strained. At least, he tried to attribute his feelings to the driving.

As the cars and lorries passed on his left, their drivers mysteri-

16

ous and distant in their cocoons of steel and plastic, Rick gazed at them. They had passed four or five black trucks already, and not for the first time he cursed the fact that Pen — (he had already begun to think of the mysterious woman as Pen, even though logic struggled to dispute this) — had chosen such an awkward vehicle to travel in. The cabs were high and the windscreens bright with the reflected sunset.

Liz knew what he was doing, he was sure of it. She had hardly looked at him since their conversation had ground to a halt ten minutes earlier, but he could tell she was fuming. Every time they passed a truck, Rick kept his eyes on it as they slowly approached. Then, once past it, the atmosphere in the car deteriorated some more. But try as he might he could not help himself. He felt miserable, frightened, alone even with his wife, the woman he loved. He wanted to talk to her sensibly about what he had seen, or thought he had seen. He wanted to be reasonable about it. In a way, he realised, he wanted her to talk him out of it. Persuade him he was wrong, tell him what an idiot he was, convince him that he had seen someone who only looked like Pen. Walked like Pen. Ran like Pen . . .

But the conversation had rapidly escalated into a shouting match. At first Liz's concerns had seemed trivial and selfish. She had been embarrassed; everyone had been looking as the car skidded to a halt a few feet from Rick. He had seemed unconcerned with all the attention he was receiving, and when a group of teenagers had giggled and mouthed some rude jokes about the bald guy in the road, how he must be mad or pissed or both, Liz had lost her temper. From that moment on, the argument was almost inevitable. One thing Liz rarely did was to let anything lie, forget it as an isolated incident. It had happened, she wanted to know why, and when Rick told her she laughed, then scowled, and then almost cried. Almost.

She would not cry, not yet, not while the tension was still there. She hated appearing weak. She loathed apologising, even when she knew she was at fault. That particular trait had caused many arguments in the past three years of their marriage that could otherwise have been avoided, but this time she knew she was right. She was right and he was wrong. Let him apologise.

Then Rick had sensed a change in her mood, even as the stress between them increased towards breaking point. Underlying Liz's professed embarrassment was something else. It was an almost frantic fear. Not, Rick thought, about whether he was telling the truth or not, for he was sure that she had already decided he was mad. This was something altogether more animal, something to do more with ownership than the human emotions of concern and intrigue. She was married to him, Rick, not to his memory of a long dead girlfriend. And it was this more than anything, Rick felt, which had driven Liz to the point where she now simmered.

And he could understand it. He really could. She had absolutely no belief in the possibility that the woman had been his ex-girlfriend; Rick's search, and his certainty that it had been Pen, seemed nothing more than a reawakening of his thoughts about her. Thoughts that should realistically have been buried years ago in the file marked personnel reference only, not to concern others. Yes, he could understand.

But that did not stop him from looking whenever they passed a black truck. Ignoring Liz as she sat distressed in the driver's seat, feeling betrayed, cold, unloved.

two

Pen.

The word seemed to have some meaning for her. It had stirred something deep inside the forbidden portion of her mind, the part that sometimes offered her tantalising glimpses of some greater certainty, but seldom, if ever, gave her the chance to guess at its nature. On hearing the name spoken by the stranger, her skin had tingled, goose bumps speckling her arms and neck, and for an instant barely measurable in anything other than memory, there was something there: a park, a warm summer afternoon, a feeling of belonging and love. Then the memory had vanished again, swallowed alive by the confusion and fear that were now her constant companions and playmates. It left a taste, a yearning for the truth that she had lived with for as long as she could remember, minutes or years. It was like a memory that had been stolen, a sense of *déjà vu* where nothing actually existed and nothing was seen — empty, meaningless, wanting.

She hugged her knees closer to her chest, keening like an abandoned kitten left out in the rain. She hardly noticed the water as it trickled from her head, through the matted strands of hair, into her lifeless, pathetic eyes, across the barren landscape of her dirty face, down into the neck of her shirt, exploring shamelessly the confines of her clothes and finding little, save for hunger and abject neglect. Following the corrugations of her ribs, the water continued on its way until it was absorbed by the bunched mass of clothes around her waist. Tattered rags that had seen better decades, and which now housed only a defeated, forgotten and forgetting body.

She rocked back and forth on her bony behind, hardly noticing the pain of the sores where her bones compressed the thin layer of flesh and skin into blisters and weeping wounds. The pain was remote, an echoing sensation which she had learned to ignore long ago.

The alley was narrow, dark, piled high with refuse from the hotel and restaurant that formed its two walls. There were others sharing the space with her, but she took no notice of them where they rolled and cut themselves on the smashed alcoholic dreams of yesterday. Occasionally she would become aware of their existence, watching unconcerned as they fought each other over the possession of a bottle or shoe, or simply fought themselves and cried and slept the sleep of the dreamless.

The girl occasionally moved, when the calling urged her. But usually, whether it rained or the sun shone or the snows tried to bury all trace of the decrepit inhabitants of the alley, she stayed where she was. She rarely ate, and when she did it seemed to her that it was to satisfy some long dead habit.

It was unnecessary, a part of her infrequent insights into the bigger world.

three

Rick s pet hate as a child had always been bath time. His mother had often been forced to pursue him around the house, searching for him in all his favourite hiding places: the musty cupboard beneath the stairs; under his parents' bed; jammed behind the freezer in the larder; sometimes even in the airing cupboard under a camouflage of towels and bedding. Even then, the search complete and the prisoner apprehended, the struggle was far from over.

As he had grown older, however, he had come to love the therapeutic properties of a warm, bubbly bath. In his teens it had been his favourite place in the house, much to the ironic mirth of his parents. He had spent hours and hours in there every week, a good old-fashioned spaceship-and-galactic-war science fiction book soaking up the damp atmosphere. Luxury. Relaxing, floating, letting his worries drift away with the condensation, collecting on the windows and walls to be wiped down afterwards and squeezed dismissively down the sink.

Even after the strange events of the day, arriving home and

finding unexpected bills on the mat and no milk for a cup of tea, the argument with Liz and the terrifying, crawling fear in his stomach as he turned the events over and over in his mind, searching for the loophole, seeking the logical . . . the bath still worked.

The hot water — as hot as he could bear, as always — massaged his tired body with liquid tenderness. It drew the fear from him and replaced it with a mild discomfort; it eased the tautness in his muscles from where he had been sitting in the car, tense and watchful, and replaced it with a comfortably dull ache, like the satisfying sensation after an energetic workout. The bubbles and bath salts did their work and sent him into a weary, light doze. Sweat tickled him where it ran from his bare scalp into his ears, his closed eyes, down onto his chin and from there to his chest. He absently brushed away the droplets of salty fluid. They returned soon after, to be swept away again.

The bathroom was heavy with mist, an effect he had come to like in his teen years. Then, it had added to the atmosphere of mystery he felt when he read and aided his enjoyment of the many books he had devoured in those formative years. He rarely read in the bath any more, finding it easier to simply lie there and let his mind wander. The glow of the light through the mist was ghostly, pale, indistinct. If he really stretched his imagination, he could picture himself lying on some tropical beach, legs and body in the water, the sun blazing down through the heat haze overhead. All he needed was some bronze-chested native beauty to wander in with a hand full of coconut oil and eyes full of promise.

Rick shifted slightly in the hot bath, causing a ripple to splash down past his feet, hit the end under the taps, curl back and run across his legs, groin, stomach. He slowly raised his hand, wiped away the beaded sweat from his brow, ran it through his rapidly thinning hair to remove the excess moisture from his scalp.

He felt the water stroking his body, and the native woman was there. She ran her fingers down his sides so that he caught his breath; he had always been ticklish, much to Liz's constant amusement. The caressing lessened until it was a happy memory, and instead the native girl, face obscured by her cascade of dark, heavenly hair, cupped his balls in her hot hands. The sand changed to grass, the mist changed to a warm summer day many years ago, and the native girl looked at him.

Pen sat on the dry, cracked earth at his side. She smiled, showing the small gap between her front teeth that he had found so sexy. He recognised the day — it was Pen's twentieth birthday when he had taken her into London to see the sights. They were in St James' Park, having seen Buckingham Palace and deciding to eat their picnic by the shores of the lake. Ducks and swans awaited their share. Pen smiled at him, her hands still caressing his balls. He saw that he was naked, but it did not surprise him. Neither did the sensation of water rippling over his body, even though he could see that he was dry, shreds of dead brown grass speckling his skin. His penis stood hard and high, Pen teasing it with quick tickles from her thumb. She knelt forward, and Rick knew she was going to do the Special Thing for him, here, in the Park, while hundreds of people watched, disinterested and uncaring. A little girl ran after her football, jumping across Rick's chest as Pen enveloped the end of his penis with her mouth.

'Nice dream?' a voice said.

Rick snapped awake, jerking up and splashing water over the edge of the bath. 'Oh. Hi.' He looked down at himself where he protruded proudly out of the receding bubbles. Sitting up so that the water covered his diminishing erection, he looked up at Liz through sore, tired eyes. 'Okay?'

'Yeah,' she replied quietly. She let the toilet seat down, sat down to pee. 'Nice bath?'

'Hmm. Lovely. Do you want it after me?' For an instant, short but complete, Rick forgot everything that had happened that afternoon — the strange events at the services, the drive home, the arguing, the feeling of guilt — then it all returned in one great, all-encompassing picture, and with it the memory of his daydream. His expression changed, his face dropped. Any benefit he had gained from the bath seemed redundant now as he watched Liz on the loo, the expression on her face. Angry. It scared him.

'Had a think about it?' she asked quietly.

'Liz . . .' Rick cringed and looked at her pleadingly. 'Come on.'

'Come on yourself,' she said angrily. 'What do you think I am? You can't just do something like that today and expect me to forget it.' Her hands were grasping her bare knees, white moons of flesh around her half buried fingertips. 'You're just being stupid.'

Rick sat up straighter, brushing the few remaining islands of bubbles around the surface of the soapy water. The silence persisted, uncomfortable, vibrating with the argument from earlier on, and the threatened continuation as yet unleashed. He really did not want this to go on, not tonight, not now. Now he was just tired, soothed by the water. Bed was calling him. They had had a wonderful weekend in *Polperro*, spoilt only by the strange journey home. Now, the antagonism between them upset him. He felt it unnecessary, unhelpful. Whoever he had seen at the service station was long gone, and unlikely to ever be seen again. He still had a strange feeling in his stomach. Maybe he was missing her, even now, after eight years.

He hated to admit to himself that the love was still there, an occasional wall between Liz and himself, but the memory of the dream confirmed it for him. He tried to ignore it, lose it in the steam of the bathroom. Willed it to float away like a forgotten puff of breath in a storm.

'Liz, honey, I thought we'd sorted all this out in the car,' Rick said in his most obsequious voice.

Liz huffed, tapping her fingers on her knees, looking at the floor. 'Oh yes, well sorted, I must say,' she said caustically. 'You finally said that you didn't really believe that girl was Penny, after insisting it was for half an hour. And then only because I was going on at you.'

'What did you want me to say?' he pleaded.

'I wanted you to say you'd been mistaken, or you'd seen someone from school or seen a film star or . . . or anything. I didn't need to hear that, Richard. I didn't need to hear you tell me that you'd seen Penny, for Christ's sake!' Liz was close to shouting now, her face red with anger, a blotchy rash spreading down across her neck and chest.

'But . . . she's dead,' Rick said lamely, questioning the truth of this even as he said it. So if she was dead, just who the hell had he seen that afternoon?

'I know she's fucking dead!' Liz shouted. 'I know, I know. I knew it when I met you, and I knew it when I married you and I know it now.' She quietened down slightly, her voice imploring, a trace of desperation mixed in with the anger. 'But how do you think I feel when you make a fool of yourself, say you've seen an ex-girlfriend of yours who's been dead for eight years? What do I think you've been thinking about her? And I honestly think you really believed it there, for a moment, Rick. And you had a hard-on.' She nodded down at his lap. 'You really thought it was her.'

He ran his hands over his face, through his hair, brain sluggish and dulled by the constant arguing and the dilemma it had been presented with that day. It was still trying to work it out. As the fogginess of the hot bath cleared from his mind, the realisation of what he had seen impinged once again on his thoughts, insisting he examine it, dissect every memory in the hope of finding the truth — that he had seen Pen today. Older. Greyer. Thinner. But unmistakably Pen.

Rick looked up at Liz, his face drawn and tired. 'Babe . . . I don't know what to say. I really love you, you know that. But I couldn't help what happened today. That girl looked so much like her that . . . I just sort of went weak-kneed and flustered for a while.'

'Weak-kneed?' Liz said quietly. 'You still go weak-kneed at the thought of her?'

Not the thought of her, Rick thought, the sight of her. I saw her. I did.

'No, Liz, that's not what I meant.'

'I'm going to bed.' Liz stood and went to leave the bathroom, her lower lip protruding slightly, eyes grim and hooded.

Rick reached out and grabbed her arm as she passed the bath. He held her, firmly but gently. 'Liz, wait, we can't leave things like this.'

'Like what?' she said in a monotone. Distant.

'Like this. Look, I don't want to argue any more. I'm sorry if I embarrassed you . . .'

'Do you think that's all it is?' she hissed.

'No, no, of course not. I just don't want to argue any more. Let's be friends again? Please? Come on babe, I hate arguing with you.' He looked at her plaintively, like a lost puppy. This had often defused a tense situation in the past, and he briefly considered whether or not he should start to whine.

'Richard, let go. I'm going to bed. We're not friends now, I'm just too pissed off for that. In the morning. In the morning it'll be all better. We'll go back to work and you can buy me some flowers and cook me a nice meal tomorrow night, and everything will be okay. Now . . . I'm just too pissed off. Alright?'

Rick knew this was the best he was going to get. She hardly ever called him Richard. 'Fine. I'll come to bed soon.'

'I'll probably be asleep, I'm tired.'

'Fine.' He watched her leave the bathroom, her nightdress moulded to her shapely hips and bottom. He found himself stirring with desire, but he wondered instantly where the feeling had come from. He had a fleeting image of a park in London. And Pen, doing the Special Thing to him.

Tomorrow. Tomorrow, in the logical light of a fresh day, everything would be all right. The memory of today's strange events would be just that, a memory. One to be mulled over at some point in the future, even laughed about when Liz finally forgave him. Midnight, and a good night's sleep, always did wonders for a bad day, casting aside its faults with a dark sweep of the hour hand on the clock, cleaning the slate, priming the engine of life for a full new day.

But the morning they were both expecting never came. The

morning when they woke up and cuddled and he apologised again
and she listened and accepted it. The morning when they made
love before going to work, as they sometimes did when things
were going well or when they both miraculously woke in good
moods. Normality, that wondrous elixir which cured life of many
ills, imagined and real, disappeared that night while they both
slept. It was swept away by the same dark hour hand that should
be marking the approach of the new day, the logical day, the day
when strange thoughts about dead girlfriends and jealous wives
and mysterious sightings of those long dead were forgotten.

A phone call came out of the dark at five o'clock in the morning. It was still only half light, the birds celebrating the approach
of another day, a safe day just like all the safe days before. Liz
sprang awake, always the light sleeper, but Rick rolled over and
grabbed the phone from his bedside table before she could reach
it.

Yesterday hit back at Liz instantly, and she felt a sudden rush
of love towards Rick. She had treated him terribly. She stared at
his back and smiled, running her hand down his spine where it
bumped the skin. Then she heard his voice, and knew that something had fled them in the night. Something good.

He gasped as he pushed the receiver to his ear. 'Pen . . .'

*   *   *

Sometimes his name was Damien, or Damon. Possibly Darren.

Today he was Damon, as he had been for nearly a year. He
wrote it down every night, often using the same piece of grubby,
torn paper for up to a month, and placed it next to him when he

slept. Wherever he was — in an old, insect ridden bed, under a bridge, in a hostel reverberating to the tunes of a dozen snores — he made sure the name was there when he woke up. This had started as an exercise in associated memory, a means by which he could save himself time by not having to remember his name every day, and instead use the energy to be able to recall other more vital facts and images. But over the years it had turned into a religion, something to grab onto as he fell asleep in another strange place with other strange people, similar to himself or not. The name was something to enclose with his mind as he succumbed to the endless plains of sleep, where what had happened to him had no significance. The name gave him identity, in a spiritual sense as well as physical, a belonging, a marking as something there, something important. A grain of sand, true, in the desert of life. But a grain which could perhaps achieve something other than mute, imbecilic existence.

Years ago, too many to be able to count, Damon had been attacked and killed and robbed of something essential. He could remember this as clearly as if it was happening before him now, the tableau frozen in his mind's eye like a still from some cheap horror film: the blood, the attackers' savage grins, his tortured face split under the continuous blows of their fists. His hands, bolted to the wall. He could see the clothes he wore — a suit, shirt and tie — but he could not remember why he had been wearing them or even whether or not they had been his own clothes. He sometimes saw the same types of attire on the people who passed him by in the street. Occasionally they stopped to drop some loose change on the ground at his feet, but mostly they drifted by on the breeze of disinterest, guilty in their ignorance.

And now, this. Another memory awakened, one that had become rusty through lack of care and stiff and ambiguous with little use. The memory of a girl, and what he had seen them do to her as he sat wasted against the wall. Unable to help, unable to talk in protest or lend a hand. He was even becoming aware that he knew what had happened — to her as well as to him — but that this knowledge had been shielded inside him for the many years between those pivotal, terrible events, and now.

He had found a cause. The girl, the one he had seen. Summers had been her name. The sun had forsaken her on that day so long ago, no natural light had aided her attackers or saved her from their manic fury.

Damon coughed, squirmed in the flowerbed where he had hidden under the bushes to sleep. It was hot, the place was still busy even though the night had been here for hours and was fast receding. He felt the earth and chipped bark finding its way through torn seams and splits in his clothes like insects bravely seeking their next home or meal. The smells of the earth and the plants mixed with those from the building, burning meat and cleaning fluids and the mingled sweat and smoke odours of the travellers who went there.

Yesterday he had seen the Summer girl. He had been uncalled, unprepared to meet her. He had hidden while she strolled aimlessly through the glass-walled buildings. He had followed her out into the open, watched as she dodged cars and was called by one of the *Normal* ones, ran from him, was whisked away into the heat haze by a lorry.

Summers, the name. Pretty girl.

The *Normal* one . . . he had looked so lost, so pained as he watched her leave. Damon had felt an instant affinity with him, perhaps because the expression on the stranger's face mirrored what Damon thought his own image presented — abandonment, longing. As the *Normal* stood in the middle of the entrance road, with impatient drivers hooting for him to move and his flustered companion trying to pull him back to the pavement and sanity, Damon had watched him closely.

He had recognised the Summer girl, that was plain in his eyes. But there had also been some doubt there, disbelief verging on awe which prompted the slack-jawed, wide-eyed stance in the middle of the mad traffic. Damon did not know the man, at least as far as he could remember. But the stranger had obviously known the Summer girl.

Damon shivered in the heat as he recalled random images from aeons ago, before history started, before trace memory began, and where real memory ended: the cellar, walls screaming at him with the unfairness of it all; grey, slimy water running slowly down from the ceiling, as if comprised of syrup, or blood; a spider as big as his eye using his leg as a dining area, dismantling a bloated fly before his terrified eyes.

His hands, bolted to the wall through cruel holes in his palms, the blood dried into black, caked stoppers.

The door opening, the Summer girl being thrown inside. Half naked, bleeding. Then, the man getting to work on her, bolting her to the wall opposite him, ignoring her screams.

Time passed, deleting memory with its tenacious ticking.

The man again, but this time with another, one of power, one of importance. The Mesmer, converting the girl to his cause before sucking everything good from her.

There, for now, memory ended.

Damon sweated back into a half-sleep, shaking the bushes of the planter, unaware of the attention he was drawing from curious passers-by. For a time it was raining on him, blood and the tears of his old self soaking through his porous skin and instilling him with new life. Then, the coming day bore through it all and woke him once more with its intervening light.

When he emerged from the bushes the small crowd that had gathered dispersed with distaste. Several of them remained and stared at him blatantly, but he soon saw these off with a request for "a few coppers for a cup of tea?"

After they had left, he reached into his pocket and tugged out the new leather wallet, *Polperro* proudly advertising itself on the front. The thought of Cornwall sent a shiver through Damon, but he quickly shook it off and delved deep into the wallet. He searched past the cash and credit cards, looking for what he had found yesterday. The business card, with the name of the *Normal*, and the telephone number.

He stood for a while with his head bowed, staring at his holed, scuffed shoes, at the socks protruding from them, at the faded baggy jeans he wore. He felt no self-pity or remorse or frustration, because he was way beyond any such basic emotions. He simply stood there like some still-life portrait, the rain smearing his forehead with errant straggles of hair. A fly landed on his nose, explored his damp nostril as a possible haven from the downpour, then thought better of it and fled.

Damon did not notice. Vague memories drifted into view in his mind, then away again, like cartoon captions lacking in dialogue, colour or life. For some time he struggled to remember what he had been about to do. He had been asleep in the bushes, he knew that, and he had been dreaming about something that had happened to him long ago. He had also been dreaming of someone else, and the memory of this thought flushed through him and reanimated his tired and cold body with a purpose.

The *Normal* one, looking at the Summer girl as she rushed between the cars, fleeing from someone or something, perhaps just running away from her memories. The loss Damon had seen in his eyes, an image that for a moment had conjured something similar within him, before reality had impeded the vision and scolded him for his foolishness. Although he knew that the man was completely different, *Normal*, part of society, Damon still felt an inexplicable urge to help this stranger. But there was no way, no possible route down which he could go in order to aid the man cure his agony. That was unthinkable. That was foolish.

The telephones were vacant, standing unused and cold and impersonal. Damon fished in his pockets and pulled out the handful of change he had collected from the previous day's begging. About five pounds, mostly in tens and twenties. He grunted, paused for a few moments, considering the folly of what he was about to do.

He picked up the receiver.

The sudden desire came over him to stop, the realisation that what he was doing could change nothing and help no-one forcing its way through his dull, clouded mind. What was he doing? He had seen the Summer girl, so why was he phoning someone else to tell them? He knew what he had seen, and it was something that could be, and should be kept to himself. It was private. It stirred memories that were very personal, even if they rarely revealed themselves to him other than in dreams or under the influence of alcohol, tiredness or depression.

As Damon decided that he would retreat back into his own small, confused world, leave those outside on the outside, keep the memory of the Summer girl and what she had gone through on the inside, he heard the ringing of the phone. He had dialled the number. His free hand fell to his side, swinging aimlessly.

Before whoever had picked up the phone could talk, Damon spoke: 'You saw her?'

He heard a gasp. 'Pen . . .?'

Damon frowned. The name was wrong, but the feeling . . . the feeling was right. The sound in the person's voice. The loss there.

'The Summer girl,' he said, and hung up.

four

Rick gently took the tray from the grill, turned over the two pieces of golden toast to reveal their white underbellies to the heat, put the tray back in. He did not want to cause a sudden crash, afraid that Liz would regard any such noise as an indication of temper. The kitchen was silent save for the inane breakfast banter from the local radio station that Liz insisted on listening to every morning.

'Drivel,' Rick said quietly. He opened the margarine, saw that it was soft because Liz had left it on the worktop last night instead of putting it away in the fridge. He hated it soft.

'I'm sorry?' Liz said from the table, eyebrows raised in disbelief.

'Nothing,' Rick responded. Shit. Now he'd started it again.

'Drivel? After all the crap you've been spouting over the last few hours? Drivel?' She plucked the spoon from her cooling tea, which she had stirred about a hundred times. She stood, lobbed it into the sink. It hit a glass, knocked it over, crashed into a mug stained with brown traces of last night's coffee.

Rick remained facing away from Liz, afraid that eye contact would recommence the argument. He took the toast from the grill, dropped it painfully onto the breadboard as it burnt his fingers. Soft margarine, no jam because they'd worked the larder down before their few days away. Great.

He spread the soft, gelatinous mess onto the toast, and suddenly he was no longer hungry. He could sense Liz behind him, waiting for an opening, stalking his confusion so that she could again prey on it and turn it against him, put him down, mock him. And why? Was she jealous? Or was she scared? Or both?

Rick turned around. 'Are you just scared?' he asked, quietly, trying to control his voice.

Liz grinned bitterly, nodded a couple of times, and went back to her chair. She did not sit down.

'Oh yes, that's it. I'm scared of fucking ghosts and ghouls, you idiot! I'm really afraid that your old tart has come back from the dead to haunt me and to take you away from me.' Her face was reddening, maybe through anger, perhaps because she knew she was losing control and she hated herself for it. Or it could be that what he said was the truth.

Rick frowned. 'Don't talk like that,' he said without any real conviction. He was not enjoying this, not one bit. It was very rare for them to argue this bitterly, even rarer for an argument to carry over from the night before.

'What? Don't you mean don't talk like that of the dead? But Richard, I thought you were sure Pen had come back from the dead . . .'

'I never said that.'

'You gave a great fucking hint at it! First you see her, then

42

someone phones you and whispers to you about her. But . . . oh, hang on a minute, what's this? Isn't this a memory in your head? Hmm, let's see, what does this signify? Large black wooden box, a field with a hole in it, lots of people crying, tears, mud, a vicar . . .? Paints a pretty grim picture, even for someone who isn't dead.' Liz grabbed one of Rick's slices of toast, but before she could do whatever it was she had in mind, it slipped from her shaking fingers. It landed buttered side down.

'Liz, come on, I can't change what I saw.' He was trying to be conciliatory, he really was. He was still in a state of shock himself, his mind an island of conservation in a sea of change. So much was different today, so much that yesterday had seemed important was no longer so. There was something here, in his head, in the phone, in his memory from yesterday in the service station . . . something inexplicable, confusing, daunting. Liz was dealing with it in her own way. Fear, anger, perhaps disappointment that Rick was seemingly pursuing something so nebulous and uncertain instead of paying attention to her.

Rick himself felt hardly there at all. His mind was conducting the argument from afar, most of his thoughts actually directed inwards at the wall of logic which he found himself even now trying to break down with bombs of hope and rams of an old love remembered.

'You bastard!' Liz screeched through fresh tears. She slumped into the chair across the table from him, her head in her hands, looking down at the scarred pine. She was trying to hide her tears, but Rick could see her shoulders moving, hear the sniffles that she tried to disguise as early morning sniffs. He saw two or three droplets of salty tears reflecting strip-lights on the tabletop.

He wanted to go to her, touch her, comfort her and tell her that she had nothing to worry about, it was just an off day. For ninety percent of their arguments this shallow excuse may have worked, partially at least. Then would come the apologies, the forgiveness, the cuddling. When he was younger, before they had married, Rick had used to fabricate minor arguments out of irrelevant subjects, just so that they could make up and make love. He had liked sex that way. It had seemed more passionate.

This was different. The subject of the row could not be forgotten so easily, not by Rick and not, he knew, by Liz. He had been talking all morning, since waking up, about an old girlfriend who was dead. Talking as if she was still alive. He had been unable to avoid the tone of affection creeping into his voice even when he was trying to explain to Liz what he had heard on the phone last night. She had suggested that it was a prank call, but could anything be that much of a coincidence? Then she said that he had dreamt it, but she herself admitted to hearing him on the phone, however briefly.

And so, stalemate.

'Babe,' he said placatingly. He walked to her and gently laid a hand on her bare shoulder. The summer dress seemed incongruous, the wrong type of clothing to wear for a row with your husband. She shrugged his hand away, and he sighed in frustration.

'What are you going to do?' came Liz's muffled voice. She did not look up from the table. Rick could hear the tears in her voice.

'Go to work, I suppose. Great, back to work. I'll have to get two signs drawn up for everyone, one saying "Yes, lovely thanks" and the other saying "No, of course I'm not glad to be back". I get sick of telling people about my holidays.' Rick grimaced at his attempt at humour, the old joke that he used after every holiday. Wrong place, wrong time. Idiot.

'Sure you've got plenty to tell them this time. Pints worth. Lunchtime storytelling, I'm sure.' Liz lifted her head with a sigh, her eyes still downcast in a vain attempt to hide the redness there. 'Go on, then. This will have to wait.'

Rick almost went to her, to tell her that it could not wait and that they had to talk about it now, sort it out now. But how could they do that when even he did not know what there was to sort out, what was happening, or what he could say to Liz to console and reassure her?

Instead, he nodded to her and said okay and turned to the door to leave. He had not made any sandwiches, but he could buy something at the shop in work. He had forgotten his tie, but could not muster the energy to go back upstairs and select one. At the back door he turned once more and told Liz that he loved her, that he would see her that evening.

'If you see Pen, tell her hello,' Liz said bitterly.

Rick looked at her, his face expressionless. Then he shut the door.

It was already warm, the morning air starting to move with the gentle breezes which had been making the recent heatwave just about bearable. The car was in the drive covered in a fine layer of grey detritus from the atmosphere. Dust from Africa, apparently. The lawns either side of the driveway needed cutting, but Rick had never been a practical man about the house. He enjoyed gardening when he got around to it. It was just that he rarely ever did.

The gate from the drive to the road was already open; another sign of Rick's admitted laziness. One hinge on each gate was broken, the metal silvered where it had split only recently. He thought that kids had probably been clambering on them. One day he would have to fix them. And paint the gates with creosote. And cut the hedges in the back garden, take up the concrete slab they had been talking about moving for three years, decorate the living room, shelve the dining room so that he could put out all his books which still resided in boxes in the attic. He rarely read any more.

Climbing wearily into the car, Rick promised himself that when he got home that night he would try to read something. Maybe some *Dan Simmons*. Or *Philip K Dick*. That had been his favourite, the one about the dreams of androids.

Pen had loved the film, too.

five

When Damon woke up he searched frantically for his identity. He panicked when he could not find the piece of paper he had been using for several weeks, and the fear made his vain attempts to remember his name even more pointless and futile. He scrabbled in the dirt, crawled from his sleeping place until he was wedged fully under a large bush, pulled the hanging branches aside, oblivious to the scratching thorns. Teardrops of blood on his hands and arms complemented the clear streaks down his grubby cheeks. He started to moan incoherent utterings of dread, his mouth open and dribbling.

His hand found a sheet of wet paper several inches from the ground, stuck in the bush. He caught his breath, the moaning stopped. The only movement was the dripping blood eager to find its way to earth. He pulled carefully, trying not to tear the paper beyond recognition. He could write a new sheet tonight, he knew that, if he could find pen and paper somewhere. All he needed after his dreamless, thoughtless, soulless sleep was to know . . . who . . . he . . . was.

Stephen, David, Dawson . . . Philip . . .

The memory, as ever, was blanked out, completely hidden. He tried to search through forgotten routes and cubby-holes in his mind, but could barely reach them any more. Where they had existed — the memories of his life, the knowledge of those who had loved him and hated him, the images of significance which his brain had so often resurrected — there was now a dull, echoing nothing.

He managed to extricate the paper from the bush's clinging arms, torn and tatty but still readable. It said: Damon. Damon. Damon. Remember it. And the Summer girl. Remember her. And 01633 746358. Remember that.

'Damon,' Damon muttered. The name felt right on his lips, if not exactly good. He said it again, louder, with more confidence. With the name came other memories, of the Summer girl he had seen yesterday and of the man he had phoned, the Summer girl's man, the one who had seen her as well.

The telephone number.

Damon hauled himself from the bushes and fell awkwardly onto the already warm tarmac of the service entrance to the restaurant. There were only a few people at the rear of the services, and the yelp he let out when he fell went unheard. He looked around guiltily, as usual, and unzipped his fly.

He leaned the top of his head against the wall, looking down as he pissed away more of his life. He had vague memories of other uses for his cock, ones that had brought pleasure. He felt a familiar tingling in his balls whenever he thought of this, but nothing else. When he had finished he kneaded his flaccid penis for a while, frowning, trying desperately to recall what he had done with it other than the act he had just performed. But nothing happened, no memory revealed itself, and he soon grew bored.

'Damon,' he muttered again, confirming the name for the day, even though knowledge of the title did not lead to identity. Not in the real sense of the word, in the "I'm Damon and this is what I do and this is what I am" way that he so hoped for. That time was long gone, the time before his encounter with the Mesmer, after which he did not know whether he was alive or dead, a human or a ghost, a wraith, an echo of a former life. Now he knew, and with that knowledge came ignorance, and with that ignorance came a sad, defeated acceptance of his lot.

He shuffled along the hard pavement, kicking a can out of his way, intending to keep it ahead of him but losing it under a parked lorry. The lights in the glassed-in restaurants flickered off, and he saw the vague outlines of the *Normal* people inside, going about their normal jobs, having left their normal homes to come here. They looked so miserable, sometimes. One day, perhaps he could tell them . . .

Before he knew where he was going or what his unrealised intentions were, he found himself at the same bank of 'phones from which he had telephoned the man earlier that morning. With the sight of the number on the piece of paper, the memory of their brief, one-sided conversation came floating back to him: the surprise in the voice as the man had answered, 'Pen?'; the fear he had felt when he realised that he was actually trying to make contact with someone, a *Normal*, a person who was more alive than him, more there. He had panicked, of course, and resigned himself to the fact that he could never really have had a conversation with this man even as he hung up the 'phone.

For a few seconds after breaking the connection he had tried to imagine the man's disappointment, but the emotion and the sense of it eluded him. Instead he attempted to comprehend the selfishness of his actions, but again the real sense of what he was trying to feel seemed hidden from him by a wall of apathy, a shield constructed years ago by the Mesmer, and likely now never to be withdrawn.

Damon stared at the glass and metal construction silently, losing himself for a moment in the straight lines, right angles, the smooth surface of glass which all shouted artificiality. This was a made thing, something that men and women physically put together with one express purpose— he tried to fathom that, and attempted to be sad at his exclusion from their world. But he felt nothing resembling such an emotion, and his head lowered until he was looking at the ground.

The tarmac was burned and had run in the heat of the last few days until it resembled the remains of a dead candle, twists and curls of melted wax hardened again naturally. Damon swayed slightly and his eyes took on a strange blankness as he stared at the ground. The shadow of a bird passed low overhead and cast its image fleetingly onto the smooth black pitch, and Damon jerked as a memory impinged itself on him forcefully, dragged up from some black place that was left over from a previous time.

The wall had faces. He could remember that, the continually changing curtain of faces that pleaded with him, begging with dead, inanimate eyes . . .

Damon looked up, realising that he had been standing in front of the 'phones for an unknown length of time, motionless, a statue of degradation. Somebody walked by, their curious and distasteful stare felt rather than seen. He was tempted to glance around, but he was suddenly certain that he would only see the face of the creature he had known as the Twin, bearing down on him with arms outstretched and a promise on his lips to bear him screaming to the Mesmer . . .

There was nobody there. Shadows that may have held a possibility of danger remained within the clutches of trees. Damon stepped quickly into one of the telephone cubicles and dug into his pockets. There were three ten pence pieces there, the remnants of yesterdays begging. They could buy him a cup of tea, maybe, if the waitress was kind today and would let him off the other twenty pence. But his need was a fallacy. He slipped the coins into the slot. The piece of paper was still wet, and he feared it was going to disintegrate fully as he tried to open it onto the small shelf in the booth. He stared at the smudged, half forgotten words where they lay uncomfortably on the torn paper:

Damon. Damon. Damon. Remember it. And the Summer girl. Remember her. And 01633 746358. Remember that.

'Damon,' Damon muttered. He dialled the number, breath held for the several seconds it took for the clinking line to start ringing. It rang four times, then stopped; a click, a tone, a voice.

'Thanks for calling Rick and Liz, we're in work at the moment, but please leave a message or an insult after the beep. Ta.'

'Ta,' Damon repeated. There were more tones, then a beep, then a whirring silence. 'Ta,' he said again. He glanced back at the paper on the shelf in front of him.

And the Summer girl. Remember her.

'The Summer girl,' he said, 'remember her. Remember her.

I'm here again today.' His isolation, his distancing from *Normal* people for years had made him fear and loath them in equal measures, and now he was trying to talk to one, attempting to arrange a meeting. He was a fool. 'Meet me. I'll tell you of the Summer girl. Here again today.' He hung up just as the phone began to beep and whirr. He looked around. He wondered where he could wait.

He was a fool.

*   *   *

Rick was pleased to see that Liz had not arrived home before him that evening. It was likely that she would be working some overtime, Monday was her busiest day and there would no doubt be a mountain of work waiting for her after their holiday. He headed straight for the kettle, and smiled as he realised how quickly he entered back into the old routine so soon after returning to work. He checked the post — bills, a postcard from a couple they had met on holiday several years ago and who they still conversed with occasionally. Some junk mail informing him that he had definitely won ten thousand pounds. He threw the junk mail into the bin and the opened letters onto the table in the living room. Liz would want to see them.

The kettle boiled. Rick had made a strong cup of coffee and sat down in his favourite chair in the conservatory, before he thought of the telephone. He had a sudden certainty as he approached it that Pen would have left a message on the ansaphone. The thought jarred him — she had been out of his mind ever since he had arrived home from work. Routine, the curse of modern life and the only way Rick found himself remaining sane, had swept all fanciful thoughts of his dead girlfriend from his mind and hidden them away. Yesterday, before the break from work was really over and while things could still happen on the spur of the moment, anything was possible. But today, once the monotony of life had sucked him back in and exorcised all thoughts of rest and random actions from his body, the thought was ridiculous, positively foolish. Until the split second before he saw the red flashing light and pressed the message button. The anticipation of hearing her ghostly voice was so sweet that he felt utterly let down when he heard the voice of a man on the phone.

Ten seconds later, however, when the message had ended, the unpredictable holiday spirit had returned. Work seemed so far away once more, and an almost childlike yearning for adventure flooded Rick's veins with burning adrenaline.

Liz would be home soon. He would play her the message, see the look in her eyes as she tried to explain this one away. Then, Rick thought, he would take a little drive.

six

Damon had been sitting outside the service station all afternoon, disturbed only once by a half-hearted attempt to move him on by some of the teenagers employed there. His legs remained crossed, his behind now numb beyond feeling, the wasted muscles in his thighs sleeping comfortably. When he went to stand up, he knew, he would suffer. His legs would awaken with pinpricks of pain, unhappy to be disturbed from their silent slumber. His bladder felt full, but he knew that he could hold it in simply by not thinking about it. He did not need to piss, any more than he needed to beg money to buy unnecessary food. It was all habit, the little remaining instinct left within him from years ago. Before the Mesmer. Before the wall of faces.

A handful of coppers tinkled into his money pot. He did not acknowledge the gift, did not look up at the woman who had left the money. He heard a vague mumble of anger at his lack of thanks, but she moved away, returning quickly to the comfort and security of her life after a brief excursion into his. He never thanked anyone. That way, he avoided contact.

But now he had tried to encourage contact. He was not here yet, the man who knew the Summer Girl, but he would be soon. Damon looked up occasionally, in case the man was standing there staring out over the car park, waiting for whatever contact he was expecting. He would have to speak to him when he arrived here, take him somewhere where he could talk about the Summer Girl, even tell him what had happened to her and why.

But the memories were vague, ghosts of thoughts that only occasionally coalesced into something recognisable, something other than a vaguely felt shadow of sorrow that his mind retained. Damon tried to prepare himself for the encounter, practising words and phrases, moving his mouth in a parody of speech to see whether the muscles there still worked. It was very rare that he had to talk, save for when the calling happened. He closed his eyes, initially to try to relax. But, with his view of the outside, normal world suddenly shut off, the logical, sensible part of his mind interrupted. Its voice was quiet, the effect barely felt after so many years, but still it was there.

What the hell are you going to say to him? it whispered. How are you going to tell him about the Summer Girl when you can barely remember her yourself? Fool. *Fool.*

He opened his eyes slowly, banishing the doubting voice back to its small home deep inside. He would figure things like that out when the time came. Maybe, if he started talking to the man and concentrated hard enough, the memories would return. Maybe.

Damon focused on the money pot in front of him. There was several pounds worth of change in the pot, silver and copper, enough for a meal in the services. But Damon did not feel like eating. It was not essential. He stood slowly, feeling the blood rushing through his protesting legs and his numb behind, and purposely tipped the money pot over. Coins rolled away in a pattern of confusion, some of them falling into the drainage grating at the edge of the road, others spinning in ever decreasing circles, looking for a way to escape. Most of the money remained in a sad, discarded pile where Damon had been sitting.

He left, walking awkwardly, limping and then dragging his left foot as the vague pain arrived. The money stayed where he had left it, until a young boy passed by half and hour later and picked it up. Every single, lonely coin.

*   *   *

It was nearly seven-thirty when Rick pulled off the motorway into Gordano services. He was tired, hungry, mentally exhausted, yet his eyes were wide and bright and held the sparkle of excitement which had been missing from them for so long.

He felt renewed; the strangeness of what was happening had invigorated him. The arguments with Liz seemed distant and somehow insignificant, and Rick did nothing to try to change this thought. He should be feeling guilty. He should be taking Liz out for a meal and telling her how sorry he was, how foolish he had been with his childish beliefs of late. He should, in reality, be putting a stop to all this, here and now.

But he could not. He wanted to believe, he wanted to meet the mysterious man who had phoned him last night, and left the message on his ansaphone this morning. He wanted to discover what he knew about Pen, or the Summer girl as the man called her. Rick had no doubt that the person he had seen was Pen in name at least. The possibility was there that it was someone else using her name, but then what about the remarkable likeness? And why the unsettled look of recognition in her face when she had seen him? No, he had convinced himself. It was Pen.

The implications had not even entered his mind, the effect that finding Pen would have on his marriage, the outcome on himself. He had tried to rationalise away the sighting yesterday, but all facts pointed to it being real. Years before, even before he had started seeing Pen, Rick had been a huge fan of what he called the Fantastic. He had read avidly the works of King to Kafka, Barker to Banks. He had consumed books, in his teenage years sometimes sweeping through three or four a week. His imagination had been fired and whatever he read only served to aggravate the flames, feeding them with new ideas and new worlds. Even then he had only been what he called a sceptical believer, wanting to believe the photos he saw of Roswell, or the grainy, jumpy film of the Loch Ness Monster, or the stories of alien abductions and satanic sacrifices and ghostly apparitions. But the truth was, nothing had ever happened to him. However much he read or saw on TV, he had no proof. He felt victimised; denied the substantiation he craved so much.

His imagination had still soared, and his enjoyment of the books so often landed him in trouble with ignorant school bullies or angry teachers, upset that he would rather read of avenging robots than the early history of the British political system. He was effectively Geeked by the people in school, the "beautiful" people as he called them. They were good looking, rich, adept at most sports. He was victimised by the yobboes, the "hard" ones who spent their time picking on someone weaker or smaller than themselves and making their life a misery for the entire time they were in school. Rick had never been physically abused, never got into any fights of any significance. But he was so often taunted and maligned that he grew used to it by the time he was thirteen or fourteen and effectively withdrew into himself.

Then he left school. His interest expanded, matured into a healthy respect for things still unknown, and a ravenous desire to discover them. His reading continued and became more varied, taking in elements of religion and mythology as well as straight fiction. He tried his hand at writing, but found that he preferred reading. He put it down to laziness, but sometimes thought he had caught some bug which insisted he take in as much written word as possible.

Then he met Pen, she died, he met Liz and married.

And he started to change, losing the childhood fascination that had stayed with him right through school and into his early twenties. Television began to impede on his life, interesting programmes at first, documentaries and natural history investigations. More and more he would find himself collapsing in front of the TV after eating in the evenings instead of reading magazines or books, and his full bookshelves became dusty with misuse.

He hated it. He hated the boxes he brought home from work, their impersonal, blank sides taunting him with their power to imprison his imagination. He hated the piles of videos he and Liz had acquired, and which shunted the books to one side in their search for shelf space. He hated the memory of the day when he had gone into the spare room with the manner of an executioner, packed the books into seven cardboard boxes, pushed them ahead of him up the loft ladder, left them to whatever damp fate awaited them. He hated it all, but it had happened, because he had done nothing to prevent it.

He smiled sadly, wondering for the first time in years how he had lost interest so quickly in something that had fascinated him for so long. He had promised to start reading a book when he got home, a promise that he had not kept. Now, again, he felt the same. He wanted adventure, excitement, a taste of something mysterious. After today, he may have it for real.

He had to park away from the main building, and his route to it was lit by burger signs and flashing adverts for the hotel which took up another part of the site. The air was still heavy with exhaust fumes, as it had been yesterday, and by the time he had reached the entrance doors Rick had started to cough. It happened every year. The hay fever was something he had suffered from since his childhood, it had cursed his youth and almost ruined his exams in the all important later years of his teens. But lately, mixed with the extreme heat and large pollution levels of the past two summers, he had started wheezing and coughing, unable to talk, even after slight exercise.

Coughing and gasping, Rick pushed his way through the glass doors into the services. Ahead of him was the restaurant, to his left the amusement area, to his right the shop. He suddenly realised that he had no idea who he was looking for, what he looked like, what he was wearing or where he would be. He had come all this way because of a disembodied voice, someone he did not know, who might have been playing a prank. Deep down he knew it was no joke, but the thought was there for a moment, and he realised how foolish he was being. The phrase wild goose chase crossed his mind once more.

He had seen Pen outside, by the zebra crossing. That was where he would go first. The person who had seen him had obviously been somewhere nearby at the time, and so lacking any better ideas it seemed like a sensible place to try to meet him. Rick stood in the fading light, listening to the anonymous banter of passing couples and families, wondering at their stories. He heard muttered oaths and inane chat, promises of sweets to the kids and whispers of love between couples. He glanced at some of the people as they passed, the thought entering his mind that this was the last time he would probably see any of them. This fleeting glimpse of people who could, given time, be friends or lovers, enemies or companions. Modern life was so insular.

For a brief moment Rick felt alone, so apart from the world he was observing. A shiver bristled the hairs on his neck and he smiled grimly.

He wondered why he was becoming so philosophical. It was usually only after a few drinks that he started musing on the point of it all, the small facts that seemed to escape many people but which for him were so often in the fore. Like a favourite film that he may only see another two or three times before he died. Or a holiday destination he liked intensely, which maybe he would only visit again another two or three times in the whole of eternity. The finality of life was very apparent to him in these moments, the fatality of it all, the futility, the hopelessness of health care when you were going to die. Quality of life rarely reared its head when he was like this, the fact that the meaning of life may be to enjoy it and get as much out of it as possible rather than mope around feeling depressed about how little of it there may be left. He so often felt helpless and hopeless, a depression which regularly manifested itself in his quiet moods, when everything was pointless.

Rick smiled again, shook his head slightly, turned back from the window to look out over the car park. He tried to tell himself not to be so morbid, so negative, so pessimistic. Liz was at home, waiting for him. Angry maybe, and upset, but she still loved him and would be there when he went home.

Rick had no doubts that he would recognise the man when he saw him. Maybe it would be the look in his eyes, or the way he was standing, waiting, or the clothes he wore. Or perhaps a sixth sense which could pick up something else, an intention or an emotion. And so he started to look.

He walked away from the entrance, towards the corner of the building around which he guessed the service and kitchen entrances would be.

*   *   *

Damon was cold and hungry, but cared about neither. They were echoes of emotions, phantom feelings that reverberated through his mind from his previous existence, hopeless subconscious efforts to return there again, to the life of work and play and plenty. He felt cramps starting in his legs and winced when the pain came, blinking his eyes rapidly to try to clear them.

It was dark, but still evening. Damon suddenly remembered a purpose. He remembered quickly that his name was Damon. In his rush to leave the damp, smelling area under the shrubs, he forgot to search for the piece of paper that he had placed under a stone before going to sleep. On the paper, his name, and his life.

But this time it appeared that he did not need it.

He saw some people watching him from behind the safety of windows as he struggled from under the bushes and dropped from the wall onto the paved area. He shrugged himself awake, dispersing the remainder of his tiredness around him in a miasma of smells — body odour, urine, death. His stomach rumbled but he disregarded its fake signals and it soon quietened down to its usual, vacant self. He strained his eyes, but still could not distinguish between the faces in the window. They may have been male or female, adult or child, stranger or — enemy. His poor eyesight only confirmed what his mind interpreted, that the people around him were faceless. They did not matter in his world, hardly took part in his existence, and to distinguish between them was as useful as marking the difference between his sleeping places. They were furniture to the domicile of his tired mind, cheap adornments to the blank wall of his life, serving no purpose, simply taking up space.

Damon began to walk, not recognising the direction but feeling that it was the correct one. The gaze of several people stayed on him, their grey suits only adding to the impression of uniformity — they all looked at him, all followed him as he shuffled alongside the building, expressions exuding distaste and a faint guilt. Damon did not glance at them as he passed. He kept looking at his feet, enclosed in tattered, holed shoes, where they marched him towards something that was frightening, but so exciting.

For a brief instant he wondered who he was and in the sudden panic he forgot his name. His hands grappled in his pockets for the piece of paper which was still under the bushes, but the name came unbidden to his mind as if projected there by someone else — Damon.

'I'm Damon,' he said, and the word felt right on his lips, and the feel of talking worked comfortably in his old, old muscles. He even allowed himself a small smile, even though the emotion behind it was shrouded in an insulating blanket of ignorance.

He approached the corner of the building around which the soft yellow glare of the fading sun streamed. As his feet arrived at the dividing line between sun and shadow, ignorance and enlightenment, he paused. What was he doing? What could he even tell the man anyway, about the poor Summer Girl who he had seen for only hours but remembered forever? What good could any of it do, to anyone?

Hopeless.

Something moved on the floor, and Damon saw a shadow approaching, slowly merging with the image of the building at his feet. He looked up, into the face of a tall, tired looking man. Damon saw in his eyes immediately the reflection of his own thoughts, the doubt, the fear. The man's eyebrows raised, his eyes widened, his lips compressed in an expression of surprise.

'Evening,' the man said uncertainly.

Damon coughed, grumbled in his throat, unable to speak for a few seconds. This was a *Normal*, someone who had never been through what he had gone through, someone who could not possibly know the meaning of pain and loss, desertion and degradation. A *Normal*. He wore a shirt and tie and trousers, he was one of the people who passed Damon by every day and barely saw him and only acknowledged him if their conscience insisted upon it.

Damon looked down at the man's hands and tried to imagine them going into his pockets, drawing out a handful of silver, dropping it into a plastic cup at the feet of a beggar . . . and somehow, the picture would not reveal itself. It did not seem right.

Then Damon looked into the man's eyes and remembered him as he had seen him yesterday, when he had watched the Summer girl fleeing in the lorry. The loss that had been there then, and the desire to know which had taken its place today, convinced him.

'You want to know about the Summer girl,' Damon stated.

Rick's shoulders fell, his face sagged with relief, both because he knew he had found his man, and also that the man existed at all and was not simply the product of his imagination.

'Yes, please,' Rick replied. 'Is it Pen, Penny Summers? Is it really her, because she . . . well, I know that years ago she . . .'

Damon backed off, frowning, suddenly scared by the barrage of questions and the possible consequences of him answering them. Rick saw the look on his face and relented, apologising, hands out.

'Wait, wait, I'm sorry. Listen, tell me your name. Huh?' Rick stood back, giving the dirty man room.

'Damon,' Damon said, and smiled. 'I'm Damon.'

'Pleased to meet you, Damon,' Rick said, holding out his hand. 'I'm Rick.'

'I know.'

'You do?'

Damon held out the wallet.

Rick gasped, muttered that he did not even know it had gone missing. He took the wallet and immediately checked the contents, quickly shoving it into his pocket in embarrassment as he realised what he was doing. He held out his hand. 'Thanks.'

Damon took the proffered hand, shook it, realising that this was the first real, intentional contact he had made with a *Normal* for years. Since the time when he was taken by the Mesmer, and tortured by the Twin, and spat out by the both of them. And it felt good.

*　　　*　　　*

The tea was cold, untouched, but still Rick continued to stir it. The silence between them had lasted since their initial, tentative encounter, and now it was becoming more than uncomfortable. But the man — Damon — seemed unaffected by it. Indeed, to Rick he appeared to be comfortable with it, as if the quietness was familiar, a friend.

Rick glanced up at the man across the table from him. Scruffy looking, but not intentionally so, like some youngsters nowadays. This man's state was borne of circumstance; he was a tramp, a vagrant, and there was no shying away from the fact. Rick felt a twinge of guilt at this, remembering how he had passed people by in the street before, ignoring the hands held out grasping copies of *The Big Issue* like they were life itself. He recalled how he usually looked at the beggars and thought automatically that maybe they were not genuine. Perhaps they had a car parked around the corner and made thirty or forty quid every day just by sitting there looking scruffy. Preying on peoples' guilt and sense of correctness. He almost felt like apologising to Damon. Telling him how sorry he was, giving him money . . . but he did not want to offend him. It would be admitting his own guilt to himself, as well as patronising Damon in front of the other diners. And he looked like a normal, unfortunate guy, who'd fallen on a bit of bad luck and who deserved a chance for something better. Not a charity case. Not someone abnormal.

Damon's mouth was downcast, wrinkles at the corners showing that the grimace was ages old. His brow, where it showed under the straggly hair, was grubby and inlaid with lines of dirt where it was creased. Around his ears and jawline Rick could see darker patches on the skin, not dirt, but some sort of discolouration or growth, a skin disease or a birth mark. He tried to look closer but Damon looked up, and his eyes . . . They were what fascinated Rick about the man, his eyes, so deep and full of potential, yet blank, void of anything, even hopelessness.

If Damon knew the way the man in front of him was thinking, he could almost have laughed. Almost.

'I've come a long way,' Rick said, 'and my wife will be worried. She won't really approve, you know?'

Damon twitched slightly in his seat, as if the voice had stunned him from some private reverie and brought him back to the here and now. He stared at Rick, and the thought that what he was doing was wrong, so wrong and dangerous and likely to start something fatal for all involved, flashed suddenly into his mind.

'I . . .' Damon could not speak, his muscles were working and the intention was there and the words were there, ready. But they would not come.

Rick stared at him. Waiting, mentally urging him on, but uneager to vocalise his frustration. With stutterers that was the wrong thing to do, it made them worse. With Damon, Rick was very much afraid it would make him less likely to talk. He seemed scared enough as it was.

'I . . .' Damon closed his eyes and felt a warmth behind them, something which approached excitement. He had not felt anything like it in years. He opened his eyes again. Looking through the restaurant window, he found he could read the number plates of some of the cars in the parking lot. He smiled. He felt the expression touching his eyes and he looked at Rick, saw the same warmth reflected there.

'I'll tell you what I know,' Damon said.

Rick stopped stirring his cold tea and settled back in his seat.

seven

Damon stared across the table at Rick, ready to say what he had brought him here to say, preparing himself to tell what was implanted within him never to tell. He felt like a bird eyeing the open door of its cage, contemplating release and freedom, but suspicious at the same time. Some birds, Damon knew, would never cross the threshold; the comfort of captivity was too ingrained in them. Others would go but return when the infinity of freedom frightened them. He was sure that he would step over, very soon now. But he also felt certain that past the open door to this immediate cage, there was only a larger space similarly imprisoned. The warder to this space was the memory of the Mesmer, and the never ending terror of what the Twin had done to him and the Summer girl. And that was a big factor in Damon's determination to tell.

Because he could see again. Purpose had brought progress. His sight was returning, and he felt more whole than he had for eight years. The very fact that he was sitting here talking to this *Normal*, who looked upon him as a fellow human, a person, testified to the

73

spirit he was regaining, the life that was leaking back into his bones. Just as it had leaked out all those years ago.

'You're the first *Normal* person I've spoken to, at any length, since I died,' Damon said. The expression on Rick's face hardly changed. There was a glimmer of something in his eyes — amusement, or disbelief — but on the whole, he had not reacted as fiercely as Damon may have feared.

'You died?' Rick asked blankly.

Damon nodded without looking at him. He shifted grains of salt on the table in front of him, making shapes and imagining faces.

Rick stared at him, musing over what he had just heard. Absurd, patently. But then there was that connection, the link that could not be denied, with Pen and this man. Pen who had died and been buried, been mourned and missed. He felt a shiver, a cold current passing through him which his grandmother would have called a goose walking over his grave. He almost smiled at the analogy, realising how apt it seemed in this case, wondering briefly how Damon would react if a wild fowl padded over his burial patch. Or had it already?

'You obviously got better,' Rick quipped.

'Not really.'

Rick gazed through the window, aware that Damon was still manufacturing shapes on the chequered tablecloth with spilled salt, but still not keen to meet his eyes in case he laughed out loud and scared off the only hope he had of solving what had happened to Pen.

'Is Pen the same as you?' he asked.

Damon looked up and frowned, his eyes distant for a brief

moment before focusing back on Rick.

'Pen. Pen Summers.'

'The Summer Girl,' Damon nodded. 'Yes, the same. Similar. We both got out at the same time when the old man went mad, so I suppose we're both at about the same . . . stage.'

Rick smiled, but the expression did not match his mood. The man was scaring him, all this talk of dying and still being there, and there was a sensation in Rick's stomach that he could not identify, let alone quell. It may have been fear, or nerves, or maybe the mystery of the unknown, which everyone feels when faced with a situation completely new and unfathomable.

'What the fuck are you talking about?' he said. It came out harsher than he had meant it, but it seemed that he had Damon's attention; he tried to press forward the advantage. 'You call me out here, telling me you know about Pen and can let me know what happened to her . . . or whatever . . . and now I'm getting some bullshit about dying and still being here, and you really expect me to sit here and listen. Well, here's the money for the tea . . .'

Damon seemed taken aback; his face was pale, his eyes wide and scared. He had crouched down into the seat and appeared almost on the verge of tears, but then he whispered, and Rick listened.

'I know where she is,' he said. 'I'm not making any of this up, this is for me as much as you. I feel more alive than I have since . . . well, for years now. If you'll only listen to me I'll try to explain. Something secret. Something I shouldn't be telling you, but . . . My body. False. Fake. A vessel of torture rather than a home. My real body rotted in a field. I can tell you . . .'

Rick lowered himself back into his seat, feeling ashamed

already at the way he had exploded. This was obviously a disturbed man, someone who evidently needed decent company, a talk and a good meal. And with all he professed to be able to do for Rick, the least he could do was to humour him.

'I'm listening,' Rick said.

Damon sat up, breathing hard, feeling his insides squirm with what he was about to divulge. Something twisted in his guts but it was a feeble sensation, and if it was meant to prevent him from talking it only succeeded in doing the opposite.

'I was killed on the same day as your . . . your lady, Pen. The Summer girl. We were both killed by the same man. His name . . . I can't remember his name, but he was the Mesmer.' Damon stared off into the distance, over Rick's shoulder, through the queue at the food counter and into the past. A squalid, damp cellar with three normal walls of stone, one extraordinary wall of death.

'The wall had faces,' he said.

eight

Rick sat back in his chair and frowned at the man over the table. He was trying to take in all he had just heard — take it in, digest it, file and sort the information in order to produce a coherent, cogent deduction from it. But nothing gelled. Not the description of the man, Temple, who had two faces in one. Not the old man, the one Damon had called the Mesmer, who was mutated in some bizarre way; a perhaps sex change subject, or more likely simply the subject of a madman's imagination. And not the outcome.

'What did Pen look like?' Rick asked. It was the first question he had put to Damon since the latter had started his remarkable story. He sensed that the telling of it was difficult and likely to be permanently interrupted if he dared pry while Damon was talking.

Damon appeared not to hear. He was staring blankly over Rick's shoulder. He seemed far away from the grotty restaurant table, where the patterns he had made in the salt were still awaiting the damp cloth of the hired help. The frown that had scarred his face since they had entered the building had vanished, and he looked almost serene as he sat motionless in the plastic chair. His head was cocked slightly in the attitude of a listener, hands resting on the table, the index finger of his right hand tapping rhythmically as if in time to some high frequency tune.

'Damon!' Rick said. 'What did she look like? Pen?' He realised vaguely that it was dark outside and that perhaps he should call Liz to tell her where he was and when he would be home. But this may be his only chance.

Damon's attention returned slowly to the angry man before him, as did the memory of what he had been relaying. He felt something that may have been a shiver run through him, and he almost smiled at the memory of goose bumps and static shocks. He did not feel either any more.

'The Summer Girl? She was beautiful. Black hair, wild, animal. I loved her.' Damon looked at Rick frankly. 'I never even got the chance to talk to her much, but I still loved her.'

Rick leaned forward over the table until their faces were inches apart. Only then did he notice that Damon had little smell to him: dirty clothes but hardly any scent of body odour or damp; grubby face, obviously unwashed for days, but no smells which may indicate thus; bad teeth, black and rotten from what Rick could see, but only fresh air where his breath should hang heavy. 'What happened to her?' he said, quietly but firmly.

'I told you,' Damon said, 'she died. The same time as me. Only . . . not as we should have. The Mesmer went mad, you see, as it was all happening. Madder than he was before, anyway. Lots got away, apparently. We were among them . . .'

'But you died? She died?' Rick was incredulous.

'Horribly. But the Mesmer didn't finish with us. Leaving us in limbo was his own particular cruelty. So by dying . . . I suppose we escaped him.' Damon looked down at the table, blew softly at the salt but failed to move it. 'If you can call this escape.'

Rick sat back in his seat, frustrated, angry and intimidated by all that he could not know, did not believe. 'I don't understand,' he said, and his desperation gave him the voice of a pleading child. 'I don't know what you're saying. You're a ghost? A what? I don't understand.'

Damon suddenly sat up straight, his eyes wide, his hands pressing hard on the table and partly lifting him from his seat. He felt something entering his mind, something not altogether alien but a presence that his body only accepted at certain times, under certain conditions. There were other shadows of death there as well, where once there should have been echoes of life, and in these shadows Damon sensed many others like himself binding and melding in a rare companionship.

He tried to talk but found that words had escaped him. Instead, he simply stood from his seat and started to walk away.

'Where are you going?' Rick shouted, rising after him.

Damon ignored him and continued strolling towards the exit. A terrible sense of betrayal cloaked his mind; a feeling that he had sold the trust which others had invested in him for no valid reason other than to satisfy a curiosity. No good was to be gained from this encounter with a *Normal*, no benefit to his fellow dispossessed other than to draw unwanted attention to themselves. With rare insight, he realised that some decade-old sense of vanity remained within him, a survivor of the death which had changed him, and which had relished the thought of contact with a *Normal*. Importance. Mattering to someone for the first time in years.

Rick clasped at Damon's arm, but his hand slid from the coat as if it were coated in oil. He grabbed again, but once more his hand fell from the arm with little more than a vague tingling where they had touched.

Damon turned around, struggled to talk. 'I have to go. The calling. I've done you no good tonight, and for that I apologise.'

'You can't go now, not after all you've told me,' Rick said. He noticed eyes turned towards them, the wary stares of the till operators wandering between them and each other as they debated whether to call for help. He grabbed Damon's shoulders, holding him still but hardly feeling anything. 'Who are you? Where is Pen? I want to see her. I have to.' Damon struggled slightly, and again Rick's hands fell away.

Damon scowled, and was somewhat pleased at his ability to show some emotion. 'All I told you were lies,' he said. 'I was lying to you, I was just wasting your time.' With that he turned and left the restaurant.

Rick shouted after him. 'I don't believe you. You meant every word of it!' He pushed through the swinging doors into the reception area and ran past the flashing, clanging machines in the amusement arcade. He caught sight of Damon's coat and followed. He reached the main doors and burst out into the cold night, but by that time Damon had vanished.

Rick stood there desperately scanning the car park, immersed in *déjà vu* as he searched the parked cars and pavements that lay around the buildings. For a moment it was yesterday; the heat haze was disfiguring the homeward bound tourists; car horns hooted impatiently, tired parents becoming progressively more bad tempered as their return to work became ever nearer; he was standing in front of the services with people looking at him, a car ready to mow him down, Liz shouting at him, Pen running from him.

Then he saw a sudden flicker under one of the streetlamps in the distance, and was shaken from his brief recollection.

Rick had always had perfect eyesight, twenty-twenty vision, something he was proud of. But even this could not help him identify the fleeing figure for sure. Then again, how many other people had reason to be running from the services, past all the parked cars, towards the road? He squinted, looked slightly to the left and right of the shape to let his night vision have full advantage. The sight that convinced him was the figure's sudden halt at the roadside, arm out, thumb raised as a lorry thundered down the ramp onto the long, straight road that led back onto the motorway.

Rick hesitated only briefly, a breath drawing in for a shout. The call never came, partly because the distance was too great, but mainly because he had already embarrassed himself once on this spot. Even though the people who had seen it yesterday were probably now at home watching TV, he did not want to hold a repeat performance by shouting his lungs out at a vague, ghostly figure. He spun around to dash to his car, intending to drive out to Damon and hopefully not be recognised until he was near enough to talk to him again. Try to convince him to stay.

Before he even had a chance to register what had happened, Rick found himself on the cold ground next to a cursing, fuming youth. The impact had dazed him, and it was a few seconds before he felt the dull throbbing in his skull that promised headaches and pain in the very near future. The kid — he can't have been more than eighteen, shaved head, his suit looking weirdly out of place — struggled to his feet.

'You alright?' he asked shakily.

Rick sat up holding his head, unconsciously checked his hands for blood, such was the sudden dawning pain. He nodded gingerly, careful not to move his head too much.

As if the confirmation had quelled the kid's shock, all politeness instantly vanished. 'Fucking idiot, why don't you take more care?' he said quietly, but with much venom. 'Dirtied my suit, look at the fucking state of my . . . oh shit!' he ended as he saw his elbow. 'Oh shit, you've only gone and torn my fucking elbow open. Look at this, you prick. This suit cost me four hundred quid, more than you make in a week, I'll bet . . . I'll have it off you, I'll sue you, just you fucking see. I've not even heard an apology yet.'

'You've hardly given me the chance,' Rick moaned, trying to stand. The kid was mourning the demise of his suit elbow, the look on his face hinting that the clothing was nearer and dearer to him than his mother and father. Rick looked over his shoulder, trying to place Damon again in the acres of tarmac. What he saw numbed the pain and urged him to stand. Damon, thumbs out, a lorry coasting towards him with its brake lights blazing.

'Look,' Rick said urgently, 'I've got to go, I'm really sorry and everything, but you weren't really . . . anyway, sorry.' He made to leave, but the kid grabbed his wrist and swung him back so that they were face to face again.

'What about my suit?' he whined.

Rick hated the sight of him, hated his voice, hated his instant referral to suing him. He despised the fact that he was young and modern and would probably cheerfully take a razor to his own arms if he thought he could blame it on Rick and claim thousands in damages. He gave the kid his best "I'm pissed off" look which he usually reserved for his meanest customers, or the kids who swung on his gates.

'I don't give a flying sugar-coated fuck about your suit, you little shrimp,' he said, conversationally. 'But I'm in a rush.' He turned and looked over his shoulder, half expecting to be struck from behind. The lorry was leaving, the lights disappearing behind a huge advert for Mars ice creams. Rick cursed, turned and ran towards his car. He heard the stunned, alarmed and faintly accusing whimper behind him.

'. . . only saying, that's all . . .'

When he arrived at his car he tried to fish the keys from his pocket and keep his eyes on the poster at the same time, as if the lorry would suddenly reappear, wagging its tail end at him like an inviting showgirl, inciting him to chase. He dropped his keys, swore again, realised that it was at least three minutes since the lorry had left. He supposed it could be up to a mile away by now. He realised that he had not seen the registration number, or what the lorry was carrying, or what it had written on its sides . . . and then slumped against the car.

'Shit, shit, shit.' He rested his head backwards, looking up into the star-speckled sky, trying to absorb everything that Damon had said and deduce whatever he had failed to say. But it was impossible. His head pounded with inexplicable possibilities.

He glanced at his watch. It was nearly ten o'clock, and Liz would be going spare. Wearily, Rick pushed himself away from his car and strolled towards the bank of telephones near the entrance to the service station.

The kid, thankfully, had vanished.

*   *   *

The woman who looked dead, moved. A startled man scuttled away from her as her arms flopped in the muck like dead fish. He reached back quickly to retrieve his mostly empty bottle, then retreated again to another doorway, mindful of the interested stares his liquor was receiving from the others.

The woman rolled onto her back and her eyes opened, seeing little, for she was all but blind. Her matted black hair, the same length now as it had been eight years ago, clasped itself to her skull like a helmet, such was the quantity of mud and filth tangled in it. A spider fell from her head as she sat up, hanging from a rapidly lengthening string of silk. It tried to crawl back up to its home, but the woman stretched her arms with a creak and the silk snapped. The spider scurried away to find a quieter location.

Her mouth opened and a high pitched keening came from within as she tried to cry out at the pain in her head. Unsure of where she was, not knowing who she was or why she was here or why the images were filling her mind like tormenting wraiths, the scream finally came.

Muffled shouts of disapproval and threat echoed up and down the alley as the sound ricocheted away between the old brick walls. She hardly heard them because she was mostly deaf as well, and she only felt the glass splinters patter over her face as the bottle smashed on the wall above her; she did not see it flying through the air, did not hear it shatter. She slowly raised her hand to her face, touched the cold skin there, squinted at it, saw no blood. But then, she did not expect to see blood.

'Weirdo!' a voice shouted from further down the alley. A shape shuffled forward, kicking split black bags out of the way, exploding showers of rubbish over the floor of the canyon between the buildings. Half-hearted murmurs of anger drifted away as the shape reared to its full height. The tramp was old, his skin pitted and creased by years of exposure to all elements. But his eyes were bright and defiant. The others knew better than to mess with him.

'Tell 'er, Daz,' someone muttered.

'Yeah, get rid of 'er. Bloody mess, bloody scrounger, weirdo, psycho. Don't want her here. Got no booze, anyway.' The chorus of disapproval swelled, then subsided when Daz approached the woman on the ground.

'You wanna' fuck with me?' he said, taking his shrivelled member from the open flap at the front of his trousers. Someone hidden in the shadows at the rear of the alley giggled like a schoolkid, but an angry look from Daz soon silenced them. He shook his flaccid organ around until it flopped into a half-hearted erection, waving it closer to the woman's face.

The woman looked up at him, saw only a vague shape in front of her, understood that the shape meant her some form of harm. There was no fear or trepidation in her as she tried to stand, but she instinctively kept her eyes on the shadow of the man before her. Her hands pushed at the wall at her back as she tried to force herself upright and came away with smears of moss and bird shit covering them.

Daz's smiled faded as the woman pushed herself from the ground. His relieved erection went back to sleep as he saw the look in her eyes . . . or rather, the lack of it. He'd used to be a learned man, a shop owner, until his wife left him and the government had forced him onto the street by giving his shop to the banks. He knew that people said the eyes were the doorway to the soul. If that was the case, then this woman was dead, as sure as his name was Daz. Her eyes were dark empty pits ready to receive the bodies of paupers, and the dusting of dead, flaky skin that surrounded them may have been the sulphur under which the unwary would be forever interned.

Daz did not speak. He turned away and walked from the woman as quickly as he could, forgetting to replace his now terrified member back into his trousers, not even hearing the giggles that he would previously have made people pay dearly for. Silently, he found a corner near the back of the alley, gathered together some newspaper pages yellowed with age and piss, sat down and covered himself.

The woman was on her feet now, the stares of her fellow vagrants sliding from her, most of them not even noticing her any more now that she was silent and Daz had gone. She staggered towards the alley entrance, where their world blended with the world of those with homes and money and clean clothes, and slowly her step became stronger. When she passed onto the pavement the difference was instantaneous. The clothes of those around here were bright and new instead of fifth hand, torn and covered with dirt. People walked with their heads held up. They were keen to arrive where they were going, as opposed to looking only at the ground in front of them, too dismayed with their lot to care about anything more than where they would sleep, what they would eat, where their next footstep would take them.

The calling made Pen turn left. The road curved around the front of fancy shops, exhorting the savings to be made today, calling in customers with large red posters and promises of quality and richness and satisfaction. Pen did not see any of this, but kept walking on, her stride now becoming more purposeful. As she left the stinking alley further behind, her face lifted slightly so that she could see vague shapes around her. She began to orientate herself, remembering landmarks like the statues at the junction of two main roads, streaked white with pigeon shit.

She knew where she was going, she was sure, but she would not actually realise it until she got there. The pain in her head had died down to an annoying niggle. People avoided her. But Pen took no notice of them, because they were *Normal*, and played no part of her life any more.

nine

His name was Temple, but his body was anything but. His teeth were black and rotten, scattered like tumbled gravestones in the cemetery of his face. They aided his work, disturbed his victims. To some they were white and fine, weapons as well as aesthetics. His hair was short and spiky, but only because this made his appearance far more intimidating. To some, he had long hair. To most, he was the Twin.

The necessity to wash his genitals or armpits had passed away with his libido, several decades ago, and so neither area had been blessed with soap since then. Occasionally they received a squirt of some cheap aftershave to ward away the more unpleasant, uncomfortable bugs, but Temple disliked the odours that people wore almost as much as he disliked the people themselves. If he had his way, their perfumed skin would be flayed from their bodies until the sweet smell of blood replaced the manufactured smells of lust, desire, pheromones. That was truly sexual.

His face — unsettling as it was and seemingly uneager to accept definition with regard to bone structure, tan or expression — was never washed. The stubble that appeared to grow from his chin, sometimes, rarely grew more than two or three days' worth without being replaced overnight by a fresh surface. The colours of his facial hair, when it did exist, varied wildly. To some he was dark, almost Mediterranean. To others the face held a distinctly Scottish tinge, the red beard reminiscent of the McGregors or other clans as depicted in old Scottish art. Other observers would swear blind that he had a blond beard, and must therefore descend directly from the Norse explorers who had pillaged so many centuries ago. In truth, even Temple had no real idea of his lineage, or how it was displayed in his appearance. He did not use a mirror, and when he had the misfortune to pass by one, or see his reflection in a shop window on a cloudy day, he saw two people.

Today the weather was cool, a friendly breeze urging him along the pavement and past a corner shop. The owner was just locking up and stared down the street, a slight frown on her face, concern already diluting into a tired, defeated smile. Two children disappeared into the distant breeze.

'Bloody kids,' she tutted at Temple as he passed. She went to say more, but her face instantly clouded over as if her eyes had, for an instant, glimpsed her own death. She worried at the lock on the door, taking longer than necessary to check that the shop was secure. She glanced nervously over her shoulder and saw the tall, broad shouldered man strolling down the street in the same direction as the cheeky children. A smell wafted under the shopkeeper's nostrils, and it reminded her of the time she had found her dog dead by the side of the road, two weeks after it had disappeared. The breeze took the memory away, and she hurried home after it in a sad, melancholic mood.

Temple turned at the corner of the street and arrived at a public telephone booth. It was one of the old red kiosks, reinstalled at the request of the local residents who had all chipped in to buy one from British Telecom. The youngsters of the area had really not appreciated the gesture, for safety glass lay scattered inside and out, and only a few panes remained patiently awaiting their doom.

He picked up the receiver with his right hand, satisfied to see that it was still connected to the main unit. He grasped the silver metal box with his left hand, and credits flashed up on the cracked LCD display. Silently, enjoying the mild static shocks he received every time he touched the metal keypad, he tapped in an eleven-digit number.

The shrill birdcall of the phone ringing at the other end of the line made him smile. He could sense the miles between the two telephones, taste the air where it flowed through the overhead lines, smell and feel the bugs where they crawled in the earth around the buried cables. Every time the ring sounded, it brought with it a fraction of the life it passed: a flock of birds sitting on a line where it passed by Exeter; a badger lying next to the road further to the south and west, blood matting in its white fur, bones gradually tearing into its lungs; a courting couple enthusiastically testing the suspension of a car parked above the buried line on the moors.

Temple sensed something stronger approaching, a sudden loud buzz of life that could only be a collection of many. Seconds later the phone was answered over a hundred miles away, and his employer spoke to him.

'Temple,' he said, although no call had been arranged, no prior time set, 'how pleasant to hear from you.' Even the impersonal phone line could barely cover the centuries his voice contained.

'Mesmer,' Temple said.

'Please, friend, how many times have I told you? I'm Maélor to you when we're not in company.' The Mesmer's voice held a note of condescension, as if allowing the Twin to call him by his real name betrothed some honour down to him.

Temple grimaced slightly. 'Alright, Maélor, apologies. How are you keeping? It's been a long time.'

'Indeed, it's been nine months now, Temple. I assume from your voice, and the lateness of this call, that you have found one of the escapees?' The old man's voice did not contain as much interest as Temple would have expected.

'I'm nearing one,' Temple replied. 'I've done the groundwork, so to speak. It's only a matter of time now before I'm led to her. The calling came earlier, very strong, a very powerful one. There will be many there. I think I know where to go. It's only a matter of time before I have her.'

'Her?'

Temple smiled. 'Yes. I think it's Summers.'

There was a pause, which lasted for so long that Temple began to think the Mesmer had hung up or the line had been interrupted. Then there was a crackle, followed by the voice of the Mesmer. 'Penny Summers?' He said it quietly, almost reverently.

'Yes, I think so.'

'So full of life, that one. A star amongst sparks.' The Mesmer fell silent again in quiet reminiscence. 'Yes, a lovely girl. A pity she escaped just before I'd finished. Such a cruel end, so near to being finished and yet . . .' He trailed off, the sound of his memories almost as loud as that of his voice.

'I can fetch her in, soon,' Temple said. 'Then you can finish what you started. Kill her completely.' His voice was full of greed, tainted with an excitement that in a *Normal* would have been purely sexual.

'You'd love to watch, wouldn't you?' the Mesmer said. 'See as I drew the last of whatever she was away from her? Absorbed her, left her hulk to fade away?'

'Yes,' Temple said plainly, 'of course I would. I always did.' He was somewhat confused now, perturbed by the tone in the Mesmer's voice. Speaking to his master after so long seemed anti-climactic, like an easy catch at the end of an exciting, invigorating chase. The correct result, but arrived at in a disappointing fashion.

'I suppose I should,' the Mesmer sighed.

'Mesmer,' Temple said quietly, 'are you alright? Have you . . . had your fill?'

'More than my fill, Temple,' the old man spoke, not bothering to correct his servant's use of his formal name. 'Much, much more than any like me in history. Did I ever tell you of my predecessor? Junod? Before your time, of course, but a person of distinct tastes, so fussy, so very picky about those he used and discarded. When I was but an infant, he said something to me which I have never forgotten. It was from a poem, which one of his victims had writ-ten as they were being held, just before he finished them:

> Greater is the man who, in the shadow of death,
> Revels in the victories of his years,
> Dwells upon the triumph of his tears,
> Smiles at his end, content in fate.

'I don't understand,' Temple said after another pause, longer than the first. 'What do you mean?'

The Mesmer breathed heavily into his mouthpiece, creating for a moment the impression of white noise, containing all possibilities, everything that could be said in one burst. 'I don't need to see Penny Summers,' he said.

'What?'

The Mesmer continued. 'I'm full. I don't need Penny. She deserves better than I can ever give her. There are many others, all around me now. I have two in the cellar, they will last for months. Penny, I do not need. She will only . . .'

Temple coughed slightly, trying to encourage the Mesmer to continue without talking. He felt that if he spoke, he would be disrespectful, and that would not do. Not to the Mesmer.

'She will only remind me. I do not wish to be reminded. I'm tired.'

That was all the Mesmer said. Temple challenged him politely to explain himself, but the presence at the other end of the line was no longer aware of the words. Indeed, it came as a relief to Temple when the line was cut and the final long tone echoed within his ear, soon ending in blankness.

Better nothing, than to hear the weak silence of the Mesmer.

Better nothing, than failure.

Temple stared at the receiver for what seemed like minutes stretched into hours. Furiously, he tried to spur his mind into action, but he could only stare at the stained black plastic, hearing replays of what his master had just said to him. The words were as real as they had been moments ago, much more than just memories, and Temple may even have been repeating them to himself.

Smiles at his end, content in fate . . . don't need to see Penny Summers . . . She deserves better . . . Greater is the man . . . I do not wish to be reminded . . .

The growl started as a thought, but quickly fled his mind to his throat, manifesting itself as something that should never have come from a mouth so small, with so few teeth. If anyone had been passing the noise would have raised their heckles, run a shiver down their spines, stomped blatantly over their graves.

What was wrong? Why was the Mesmer acting this way? Giving in, defeated, tired . . . no, it was not possible. After all the things that Temple had done for the Mesmer, from the very first crime to the most recent . . . all for nothing? All so that the old man can finally tire and start to regret, repent for the most hideous crimes imaginable? No. It was not that it was not possible, because Temple knew of other Mesmers who had gone the same way, weakened, finally drifting into a terminal depression that took their henchmen straight to hell with them. It was just not acceptable. Temple had not come this far, done these things for nothing.

Even if the Mesmer, the fool Maélor, had given in, that did not mean that he had to as well. Because he knew nothing else. All his memories were of the Mesmer and what he had done for him. Fleeting recollections blotted the quiet suburban street from Temple's view as he recalled some of his treasured moments from the past:

The man from France all those years ago, who had come to the basement with Temple expecting some homosexual sharing. He had stripped and bent over, kneading his own cock in anticipation, and Temple had giggled as he approached him. The man had laughed himself, but the laugh had strangled in his throat as

Temple's hand clasped his scrotum from behind, twisted, pulled . . .

The girl called Mary who had pretended to understand the Mesmer, been keen to write a thesis on him, had even wooed him in her own strange way. But then the Mesmer had taken her, all in one night, the quickest he had ever been. By the morning, the girl was a husk, her pens protruding from her body where the Mesmer had pierced her skin, her pain adding to his gain . . .

The time when they had been discovered by the farm hands, bleeding the life from one of the farm boys. Temple with the pitchfork, twisting, slashing, revelling in the blood that drenched him and turned the hay to a warm, velvety red . . .

All over. The Mesmer had weakened, forgotten the past glories that he had shared with Temple. Forgotten the atrocities he had carried out, even seeming to regret what he had done to the Summer girl.

Temple's growl came again, but this time it would not subside. This time the anger burned within him, a white hot pain in his chest and behind his eyes that he knew must be vented, or burn. He glowered about him, wishing he could see someone on whom he could expend the terrible potential within himself. The street was deserted. With blinding rage he smashed the receiver down onto the phone box, hand flashing up and down a dozen times in quick succession. With each crash of plastic against metal he snorted his anger, splattering the booth with droplets of saliva and snot. The receiver broke apart in his hand and he punched the remainder of it through one of the unsmashed panes of the booth. The glass shattered into a thousand diamond shards, each of them reflecting Temple's aggression as they spun crazily to the ground.

He pushed the door open so violently that it swung back and jarred against him as he left the telephone box. He cursed and stumbled slightly, regained his balance, twisted the door from its rusting hinges with a mighty wrench and threw it to the pavement.

In his mind, still the images paraded, mocking him with their uselessness, tempting him with their elusiveness now that the Mesmer had changed. Flashes of red lit the monotone pictures, the blood and pain of his victims lighting up his thoughts like the smile of a child to a parent. He smiled himself, the brilliant white, rotten brown of his grin potent with power, eager to discharge itself on someone. His right hand was throbbing with the energy contained therein, pulsing brightly as he pummelled it into the rapidly disintegrating telephone box.

Caution, the part of himself that he hated for its cowardice but which had saved him from many threatening situations in the past, reminded him of its presence. He cursed at it, driving its chicken-shit whisper back into the depths of his foul mind with growls of despair and fury, flinging his hands and arms and feet again and again at the red metal box. He caught a vague glimpse of net curtains twitching across the street, and caution tried one last time.

'Fuck off!' he screamed at the houses across from him, crying at those occupants who watched and those who did not. His voice was deep and resonant, and it carried way across the street, through windows and doors and into the minds of those eating tea or watching television.

Flashes of red again, fuelling his lust for his life, his existence, his meaning.

The Mesmer, dark in his memory, once honoured and respected, but now, even so soon after the conversation, reviled and spat upon.

A flash of red on the Mesmer, not a memory but a craving. Temple calmed for an instant as the picture formed itself from his desire, coalesced into an object of lust, the Mesmer bleeding the blood that he could not bleed, the life he did not own fleeing him to the accompaniment of his groans.

Temple smiled. He stepped into the road as he heard the smooth roar of a large car approaching.

The thud sounded like a bag of cement hitting a concrete floor. The screech of brakes followed, screaming their shock into the already disturbed street even as the limp figure was hurled a dozen yards across the road into a timber telegraph pole. The car skewed sideways, the driver too stunned to try to halt the skid. It mounted the pavement and bounced back onto the road, an explosion of bricks and dust marking its impact.

Net curtains fell back into place as hands reached for telephones.

The silence that came to the street was a holding of breath, a cautious pause in readiness for more screaming, and more madness. Even the birds seemed to have quietened for a moment, but they soon started up again, singing themselves towards night. The car's skid marks divided the street in two.

The crumpled body at the base of the pole twitched. A high-pitched giggle, quiet and excited, came from within the torn and bloodied mass of clothing. Nobody heard.

A screech of malformed metal brought noise back to the street as the driver of the car forced the door open. He climbed shakily from his vehicle, legs wobbling noticeably, crotch wet with piss. His suit and shirt were darkened at the front from where his nose had hit the steering wheel and split at the bridge. He did not seem to notice. His eyes were drawn to the jerking body across the street.

Even though it was the last thing in the world he wanted to see, the driver hobbled over to the man on the ground. The man he had killed. He whimpered as he approached, the shock of what had happened effectively deadening any pain he should be feeling from the cut nose or the whiplash or the network of cuts on his face. The sight of the man deadened everything, including his voice, and held his breath in check.

He heard a front door open somewhere and somebody shouting, but the driver could not understand what they were saying. The words were clear, the voice near, but the meaning was elusive, hidden as it was under an all encompassing terror.

The body at his feet did not look as bad as he had imagined. The guy was dead, that was plain, and something had happened to his face, something . . . disfiguring. But there was not much blood. No guts or organs or smashed flesh to haunt his every dream for the rest of . . .

There was something in the man's hand. The driver bent down, shock now in temporary control of his mind and body, and carefully lifted the flap of torn overcoat that covered the man's arm. There was something moving down there, something shifting, squirming its way from under the body where it was crushed.

The dead man's arm shot out from under him even as he sat up. The eyes opened, the mouth cracked into a smile, and Temple spoke. 'What are you afraid of?'

The driver's jaw fell open, not with surprise at the miracle recovery of the man he had just run over, but at the sight of what lay in his hand.

'Oh God!' a voice screamed from down the street. Footsteps pounded, a door slammed shut.

'What are you afraid of?' Temple repeated, enjoying the terror in the man's eyes as his worst fear revealed itself on Temple's hand.

The moth was the size of a paperback book, its folded wings the covers, its pages written with every fear the man had ever felt. Stunned beyond comprehension, eyes wide, mouth dribbling and gibbering, he turned and darted away from the horror in front of him. He ran out into the road, past his crashed car where it sat with its engine still ticking over, bouncing off the wall next to the wrecked telephone box and diverting back into the street. He staggered towards the end of the road in a diagonal. Temple stood, brushed himself down and watched with interest as the man reached the T-junction at the head of the road. In the madman's mind, he knew, was the certainty that moths as large as books were blinding him with their wings, dusting him with their thick legs, flapping around his neck and eyes, biting, biting.

The man ran in front of a bus. Temple smiled in satisfaction as he saw him pistoned forward into the path of another car. He even saw the car jump as its wheels ran over the squirming shape in the road.

He looked around, barely conscious of the shouts and calls coming from way down the street. He saw the curtains twitching again, sensed the shock in the minds of those who watched him, and revelled in it. Telling caution to go fuck itself one more time,

Temple climbed into the battered car. He was pleased to find that the thing was still driveable. Otherwise, all this would have been for nothing.

Well, except for the enjoyment, he reminded himself. Don't forget that.

eleven

Damon reached Cheltenham in the early hours of the following morning. The first truck that stopped for him, back at the Gordano services, had only been going as far as the M4 junction, then westwards towards the Severn bridge. Damon had gone with it and was dropped off on the motorway verge near to the Severn services. He had found his way onto the exit road from the services by instinct, stuck out his thumb without considering what he was doing, climbed into the back of a transit van with hardly a mumbled thanks for the benefit of the driver. His mind was on other things.

He was vaguely guilty about the way he had left Gordano. He had been talking to someone, he was sure, someone *Normal*, but try as he might he could no longer remember what they had been talking about. The suspicion that he had been conversing at any length with a *Normal* unsettled him. It was not in his nature, it was not part of his makeup to talk unnecessarily with others, and he knew better than most that discovery of his kind would bene-fit the cruel ones who had created them. His inner vision, pulled further downwards to the point of catatonia, allowed for no serious consideration of past events. They were always there, a grey fog of memory on the sea of his existence. But if he ever tried to recall them he invariably lost his way, and had to withdraw again to the here and now.

He had heard the calling. He thought that was the reason why he had left whatever had concerned him at Gordano in a hurry. He was used to hearing the calling, had answered it several dozen times in the last eight years or so, but the blanket of ignorance it inevitably draped over everything else left a somewhat resentful taste in his mouth. He was usually aware of what he was, conscious of the fact that dead should mean dead, not wandering the byways of Britain, but he still hated the feeling that he was not his own. Something else had power over him.

This calling was a powerful one, almost irresistible, begging obeyance. It did not use words or pictures, images or directions. It began deep inside, so far down that its origins were even more vague than his life before the Mesmer. Where sensation still existed it rippled through him like a mild electric shock, but slower; starting in the pit of his stomach, working its way out through his internal organs, upwards towards his head, down his legs, along his arms until it left his extremities with such a tingle that it was a wonder that blue sparks did not flicker from his fingers and toes.

He tried to investigate it, probing its meaning with his limited mind, sensing and storing everything he felt when it was upon him. But the calling denied classification, shrugged off the tendrils of his thoughts with contempt. Instead, it drew him away from wherever he was at the time and led him elsewhere, not showing him where he must go, but letting him know when his direction was right. Thus, in his slight diversion in the truck towards the Severn bridge, his limbs and guts had ached fiercely, more so the further he went away from wherever it was he was meant to be. He held out, however, because he knew that the chances of being picked up on the motorway itself, rather than at a services station, were too remote to even consider.

Cheltenham was his target. Even when he arrived there he did not know the name of the town, had little interest in it, but knew from the way the streetlights sprayed over the rear windows of the van, from the constant bumps as they drove over sleeping policemen, that he was in the right place.

The van stopped at a roundabout and the driver called over his shoulder. 'Here you are, mate. Cheltenham, city of . . . Chelts. Lots of nice students about here, if you want that sort of thing.'

Damon scurried to the back door of the van and opened it from the inside. 'Thanks.'

'Slam the doors after you, mate. Have a good one!'

The van pulled away, leaving him standing on the central island of a small, overgrown roundabout. Damon looked around, feeling the twinges in his arms and legs almost vanishing. He headed off down a partly lit street lined with huge, high houses set back from the road on either side like waiting giants. His footsteps were unusually loud on the midnight pavements, echoing back and forth across the street, chasing each other into the dark. The sensation in his stomach disappeared almost entirely. Damon relaxed for the first time in several hours, still not certain of where he must be, or why, but sure now that wherever it was would soon be made apparent to him.

A cat sauntered across the street ahead of him, hardly visible in the weak light from the tall streetlamps. The creature stopped in the middle of the road and stared at Damon, tail curling low and slow, breath misting in the air around its nose and mouth. Damon halted as well, staring back at the creature. Once, this would have scared him, he thought. Years ago. Now, he felt more akin to the creature than frightened of it. As if sensing this the cat went on its way, searching for whatever prey it stalked during the sleeping hours of its ignorant owners.

Damon came to a sidestreet; small, rutted, badly maintained. It was consumed by an impenetrable darkness, compared to the relative brightness of the main road. He could not see whether it led to a house, or into nothing.

It seemed to be the sort of place he should be looking for.

The calling agreed with a subtle, not unpleasant twinge as he started down the road, leaving Damon feeling mildly satisfied. The darkness soon closed fully around him, trees and shrubs shielding the ghostly glow from the streetlights back on the main street. The dark did not bother Damon, because he knew that whatever was in it could hardly hurt him any more than he already had been.

The ground soon became wet and soft underfoot, and Damon guessed that the potted tarmac of the road had given way to dirt. As he continued further down the track he began to sense something ahead of him, a blankness in the dark, a sort of negative area where the life signified by the abundance of bushes and plants around him — the insects, the birds, the small rodents and cats and squirrels — had been removed and replaced by something far different. It was the place Damon was seeking. A place of death and gloom, despondency and submissiveness. It left a black hole in the darkness that Damon could sense, and even though the feeling it inspired was one of sadness and loss, still he finally felt at home.

The building, when he eventually reached it, was in such an advanced state of dilapidation that Damon wondered how it was still standing. It had once been white, and so it stood out from the dark with a ghostly glow, reflecting light from the moon and the general light pollution above the city. Its windows were missing, leaving blank holes like eyeless sockets in a sad face. It was a large house, two floors, probably with four rooms fronting each floor, a couple of dead window frames to each room. Its gutters hung down from the eaves like arched eyebrows, most of their fixings long since rotted away. Water dripped from the roof and splashed in a steady line along the front of the house, and Damon could just make out where water had, over the years, worn a shallow dip in the concrete slabs bounding the building.

He approached the black hole where the front door should have been. A disinterested face stared at him from the nearest window to the left of the door, an Asian youth who looked older than anyone Damon had ever seen. Damon had seen him before, at several other callings, although he had never spoken to him. People did not speak much, at these events.

Just outside the blank door opening Damon halted, frowned, glanced back the way he had come.

He had felt the wet mud seeping into his worn old shoes.

He had seen the cat in the semi-darkness, a carrion creature slinking through shadows, well hidden.

He had heard the abundance of small lives inhabiting the undergrowth around the dead house — rustlings, calls, the sudden frantic finale to a night-time hunt.

He looked at his hands. Squeezed them together, feeling his nails digging into his palms. Almost hurting.

An expression that may have been a smile tested itself on his face. It faltered for a moment, then returned. He could feel, see and hear things in a way that he had been unused to for years. The realisation brought sudden, shocking understanding of the reason, and the return of hidden memories.

He remembered Rick and the conversation they had not finished.

He remembered the escape, during one of the Mesmer's bouts of madness, while the Twin had been away enjoying whatever foul deeds he undertook when the Mesmer was recovering.

And he suddenly knew that Pen would be here, now, in this building.

Purpose had given him a semblance of life.

The inside of the old dwelling lived up to everything the outside had promised. Patches of damp splashed the walls in the hallway, as if distributed from a swinging can by a careless decorator. The remaining wallpaper hung like dead skin, loosened by decades of damp and disinterest, piled on the floor at the skirtings in many areas like a leper's loss. The ceiling was black, the reason for which Damon could not make out. It may simply be that the previous inhabitants of the house had chosen to paint their ceiling the colour of night. The smell that hung in the air was a mixture of many things, all mingling to form a sensory manifestation of age. Damon thought he could smell the decay of a dead thing there, something he had smelled before, many years ago. He wondered whether the thing was human or animal, but the answer seemed irrelevant. Elsewhere he could sense the vile, acidic aroma of recent human habitation — piss and shit and the sweat of bodies unwashed and uncaring. The smells were stale memories of past lives; lives that had moved on from here now, either by chance or having been forced out when the first of the dispossessed arrived for the calling.

Damon walked along the hall towards the doorless opening at the rear of the house, where he guessed the kitchen to be. He ran his hand along the wall but withdrew it quickly, shocked at the amount of sensation he had in his fingertips. The wall was uncomfortably warm, as if the dank moisture dribbling down from its hidden head was the sickly sweat of the house itself. Damon stared at his fingers, scraped away the black decay which had attached itself from the wall. He had really felt something then, sensed the roughness of the old plaster under what was left of the wallpaper, the ripples of wet paper rolling under his fingers as he moved them across the wall, the strange, thick warmth of the moisture there, both on the surface and in the body of the wall itself. He thumped the wall suddenly, fisting his hand and pistoning his arm forward. His hand punched half an inch into the wall and moist, rotten plaster showered out. But it was the pain that made Damon cry out, the unaccustomed discomfort that bit at his knuckles and jarred up his arm from his injured hand. True pain he had not felt for many years, since he had been a victim of the Mesmer.

Damon realised then, with complete certainty, that it was not only his touch that had returned. The smells that he was trying to exclude from his mind were powerful, not the faint whiffs he had been used to for years. Most of the other callings he had been to had probably been held in places smelling far worse than this, but he had not noticed them. He looked about him in wonder, feeling the first faint pangs of guilt at being here, starting to reason, however unconsciously, that he no longer belonged fully with the others who were here now.

Soon, if he did not take care, he would start thinking that he was still alive.

In the room at the end of the corridor there were several dispossessed. They sat, silent and still, leaning against the mouldy tiled walls of the old kitchen. Their presence did not lift the feeling of age and decay from the room; if anything, their pale, drawn faces and distant eyes added to the sense of death that permeated everything in the house. They were mannequins, sitting patiently in the storage room of a shop, awaiting the arrival of a dresser to bring them to life. In this case, however, there were no dressers on their way, no life to bring. Occasionally one of them would move, shift a leg or an arm or slowly turn their head to look unseeing in a different direction. But these intermittent movements only went further to reinforce the whole image of the room and the miasma of death and despair that surrounded it.

Damon knew these. They were the lessers, the group of dispossessed who had been bled so close to the point of total death by their respective captors that any trace of normality had left them. It was only the fact that they had escaped that made them dispossessed at all. Another day or half day of captivity, and they would have been finally killed. They were beyond hope of any kind. Hopeless.

He prayed that the Summer girl was not one of these, but even as he glanced nervously at their blank faces he knew that he had nothing to fear. She had been at the services for some reason other than a calling, and she had run, and she had almost recognised a face from her life, from her existence before dispossession and par-tial-death. That separated her from the lessers as convincingly as death separated Damon from Rick. He was glad when he turned and left the room, but guilty that he could do nothing to help them. He could not kill them, because they were already dead. He could not talk to them, because they would not hear him. He could not sit amongst them, because any lengthy closeness to any-one less dispossessed of life than themselves caused them to become agitated and uncomfortable, thus increasing their suffer-ing. He could only turn and walk away.

Damon went though the house in his search for the Summer girl. In every room he sensed the powers of life returning to him. He could smell more, and so eventually he had to cover his nose with a dirty sleeve, much to the puzzlement of some of the observers. He could see more, although he wished he could not, for never had the usual collection of misery and despair appalled him as it did now. And he felt more. Not only physically, but emo-tionally as well. The gentle disquiet he had sensed on entering the building mutated, by the time he had reached the first floor, into a raging anger directed at the Mesmer who had caused all this suf-fering. His Mesmer.

Maélor. He could even remember his name.

On the first floor, at the end of the dank dark corridor in a room overlooking an overgrown garden, Damon found three dis-possessed sitting together, two men and a woman. Occasionally one of them would talk, whisper inane inconsequentialities that hung in the air like bad jokes. The others would listen, nod or shrug or raise their eyebrows, and more often than not forget to answer. The woman was Pen. Damon saw this as soon as he entered the room, and the knowledge promoted a vicious memory to stun him into a kneeling position, hands clasped to his temples as if trying to tear the terrible recollections from his skull:

The Mesmer stood over the prone form of Penny Summers, his naked body dribbling sweat as his muscles twitched and spasmed. The proboscis that passed as a penis, rooted between his legs but not possibly belonging there, was attached to Pen's head, drawing it close and jerking it intermittently in a grotesque parody of oral sex. He turned his head at Damon's breathless screams, glared at him angrily where he lay bolted to the wall and unable to move, to help, even to shout his rage and disgust at what he was watching.

He felt the wall twitching behind him, memories of many of those who had been here before calling for recognition but receiving none.

Maélor spat at him, turned back to the grey form of Pen's body, clasped his hands behind her head and pulled her face into his crotch. He grunted and stared unseeing at the ceiling, and Damon saw the power filling him, saw the muscles of his back tensing and flexing with their new-found life.

When he went soon after, Pen was slumped to the floor, so close to death that distinguishing her state as alive seemed pointless.

Hours later Maélor returned for more. It only lasted several minutes this time, but by the time he had finished, Pen was gone. But still there.

Damon felt a stupid flood of relief when he opened his eyes and saw the black, hanging remains of a timber ceiling above him. He was still in the house, it smelt of piss and hopelessness, but he was away from the Mesmer and the Twin. Traces of the memory remained like the aftertaste of sickness, but a smile tugged the corners of his mouth up with simple relief.

The three dispossessed were staring at him in surprise. He was glad to see so much knowledge in their eyes, pleased to notice the sharp contrast between them and the lessers who sat immobile in the kitchen downstairs. It may make what he wanted to do that much easier.

'I'm Damon,' he said. He received no reply, neither did he expect any. Names were probably meaningless to them, echoes of a past life barely remembered. He walked across the room and sat next to them on the dirty floor, their eyes following his every move.

'You're the Summer girl,' he said to Pen. 'Penny Summers. I've got to talk to you about some things.'

Pen stared at him, frowning, and the shape of her own name appeared on her lips.

twelve

He is an angel. The floating is a serene experience, but it is not important. The tingle of divinity in his arms, legs and chest pleasures him, but its relevance is not the most significant emotion he feels at present. It is the benevolence, the compassion that swells his heart when he spies a moving form on the ground below him, a strolling couple, a working man, a woman walking in the park. He feels no menace towards them, has no desire to hurt or kill them, or worse.

He floats gently down through the clouds, enjoying the moisture that collects on his pearly skin and trickles off as it condenses. For a moment the saturated air hides the land from his gaze, and he is certain that when he sees it again it will be as a stalking ground, not a place of healing. But then he breaks back into the brightness, is soon warmed by the sun shining at an angle under the cloud cover. The people are there, and he still wants to love them, help them, protect them.

He passes over a park, revelling in the positive emotions that drift up to him on the breeze: love, joy, and happiness. The people below are here to relax, to roam free, unhindered by the threat of death or disease. For a few brief moments they are immortal. He drifts lower, and a couple strolling arm in arm sense his approach. They look around in confusion, then glance up with their expanding perception. They see him where he smiles at them, exuding waves of love and charity as he lowers himself down onto the ground.

The man screams then, long and loud, a desperate sound from deep within, way beyond the possibility of acting. His eyes widen and turn black as the woman joins him, her scream starting quietly and building to a deafening, soul shattering crescendo.

He cries out, tries to tell them he means them no harm, but they do not hear. Their fear is too loud.

*   *   *

He jerked awake, the screams staying with him. Fragments of his dreams were already fleeing like startled fairies, but the feeling was still there, as was the knowledge that it was unattainable. The screams continued from the basement, hopeless howls for help and clemency. He tried to shut them from his mind, but even if he could close his ears the memory of them would combine with those of so many others over the decades, and the scream would be never ending.

Maélor sat up in his bed. His head ached, his eyes were puffy and sore, his muscles were stiff and weak. He had not had a feed for nearly three days, since before his phone conversation with Temple. The need was there, he felt it every waking second, and in his sleep he smothered it with dreams of the Maélor that could never be. But the desire was waning. Like a soldier sickening of the war, Maélor was becoming tired of the torture. He groaned out loud when the first waking pangs hit him, niggling itches in his stomach and chest. He knew that later they would worsen. Later, when he began to struggle against his instincts, his head would throb, seemingly ready to burst with the need to feed.

More screams from downstairs. They were in pain. Years ago, Maélor would have enjoyed the sounds of agony and fear reaching him from the basement. They would have been the lullaby to send him to sleep, the pleasant background music when he chose to relax or simply sit back and think.

Maélor turned slowly and walked to the doorway that led out onto the landing. With every step he took the screams became louder, more insistent. He felt a pang in his groin, a desire in his mind, but a sense of disgust and plain boredom overcame him, and a feeling of such intense hopelessness that he very nearly propelled himself forward and over the balustrade there and then.

He reached the entrance to the basement without really remembering how he had come to be there, or what his intentions were once he had opened the door. He let fate guide him, fighting the pervading sense of gloom that had taken hold of him. Years ago, he remembered, this moment — the calm before the frenzied storm of feeding — had given him one of the greatest pleasures imaginable. Now, it was a pain. Almost a torture.

The door swung open and the screaming stopped as the two naked, pathetic people inside turned to look at him.

The man was petrified, and his bowels loosened as Maélor hobbled down the steps. He was against the wall, which shimmered and shifted with the power inherent within. The woman was on the other side of the room, where Penny Summers had been. And like Summers, she was still. Fate held no surprises for her.

It was because of this, the look of calm acceptance on her face, that Maélor killed her first. He sliced the knife quickly from beneath his long coat and a red line appeared on the woman's throat. A flame of surprise burst in her eyes for the moments it took the blood to leave her, but she made no sound.

The man was screaming again.

Maélor approached him. 'It's kinder this way,' he said, not really expecting the man to hear him, but feeling obliged to try anyway. 'It won't hurt. I could hurt you . . . do you want me to hurt you?'

The man screamed. His eyes held no understanding of the words, only an awareness of madness, his own pure, terror induced insanity.

'It's kinder this way,' Maélor said, more to convince himself than with any thought of comforting the man. He swung the knife again, hacking three or four times to make sure. The man did not die quietly.

thirteen

He awoke from a stinking dream that instantly vanished. The memory of it remained, however, an odorous, sour taste in his mouth, a dark stain on his mind. The Twin did not care, could not hope to draw any conclusions from the random travels his mind took when he was asleep. It was how he liked it. He was, after all, more than one. And a man with so many terrors inside to show the unwary was bound to feel them overflowing, on occasion.

Temple sighed, and smiled, and started the engine once more. There was little traffic around at this time of night. A light rain drifted through the smashed windscreen, soaking his face.

He clicked the radio on and a happy voice told him it was early morning. He turned the voice off with a quick snap of his fingers. 'I'll tell you what scares you,' he mumbled at the radio. His earlier anger at Maélor had diluted somewhat, but still burned him deep inside like a fresh wound. The sense of betrayal was inescapable, and the pleasure he should have felt from contacting Maélor after so long was sorely missed. In its place, there was only bitterness. The Mesmer was finished, of that Temple had little doubt. But he would not be dragged down with him. There was still room in the world for Temple, even if Maélor had decided that his time was over, and he was not going to let the old man ruin his prospects by going soft.

Temple had seen it before. He had known one other Mesmer in passing, a Frenchman called Gevan. After the second world war, during which the Mesmers had enjoyed unparalleled freedom in their choice of victims and location of feedings, Gevan had withdrawn into himself, refusing all outside influences, killing his henchmen. Maélor had tried to visit him, but Gevan had driven him away with veiled threats of revelation to the authorities. He had turned into a weak, shrunken, despised old man, who had only survived for a few years because of the rats he fed from and which, in the end, drove him insane. Human lives, Maélor had always said, were the richer.

And now Maélor was turning the same way. Weakened, by whatever ill-conceived notions of morality had developed within his warped, diseased mind, he had stopped feeding. He had even taken pity on an old victim.

Temple had plans. He had plans the likes of which he had never dared conceive previously. It was as if the fall of Maélor had given his once controlled mind free reign, and now it was revelling in its new found freedom, creating schemes and convoluted methods for his own rise. And rise he would, from Maélor's murderous gutter-rat to a power in his own right. He had always resented the feeling that Maélor instilled within him, the sense of uselessness, the disdain with which he was perceived. Maélor had treated him much like any other of his conquests, though he was vastly different in almost every aspect, but until now Temple had rarely felt the desire for a free existence of his own.

Now, Maélor was vulnerable. Still a mighty power, no doubt, but breakable. Temple would make him beg. He would extract payment for the dozens of years he had worked for Maélor, bring a new respect to his life. He was going to show Maélor what he was missing. He was going to show him the feeble creature who had seemed to prompt his decline.

He would show him Penny Summers, in all her shattered glory.

*   *   *

'Do you remember?' Damon asked.

Pen frowned into the dark, the impact of everything Damon had just told her still only hinted at. The name first, the name had prompted something (Pen, is that me, Pen?) and then the story behind the name had been told, and that too had encouraged something to squirm in her mind. A hidden life was slowly uncovering itself in the detritus of Pen's new, meaningless existence. It shook off all the trappings of sleep and shivered in the cold light of reality. And it hurt. It hurt because for years she'd had little cause to think, only to exist. It hurt because her brain was used to slumber, to blank input and dismissive output, to signals that said "leave alone, ignore" rather than thoughts that stimulated excitement, and even hope. She shook with the pain of it, but still it felt good.

Pen looked back at Damon. 'Pen?' she said.

'That's you,' Damon said slowly, as if talking to a child. In a way that was true, he knew, although a child would have a learning capability expecting to be taught, whereas Pen . . . Pen may be long gone. Lost to hope.

'Me,' the girl said, as if the very concept of self was alien.

'Do you remember Rick?' Damon asked.

Pen only frowned, but the frown was deeper, and the expression on her face more pained, more human.

'Rick was your boyfriend, before the Mesmer took us,' Damon began

'Us?'

The question surprised him, as did the new look on Pen's face. The eyes were no longer blank, but sparkling with the light of discovery.

'I was with you in the cellar,' Damon said. 'I saw what he did to you. He did the same to me, then we were no longer there. We escaped. I think . . .'

'I can't remember,' Pen said. 'I can't remember you, I can't remember this Rick. I can't remember . . . myself. Only an alley. Dirt. Scum. Cold.'

'In time, it will come back,' Damon comforted her. 'Days ago I was the same, and now . . . I feel . . . well, alive. Like new.'

'How?' she asked.

'I spoke to Rick. He saw you days ago, has been looking for you. He found me and spoke to me, and speaking to a *Normal* did something good to me. I think it encouraged me to remember what my mind had been holding in check for so long.'

Pen looked down at her hands in her lap. A dozen emotions vied for supremacy in her mind; anger at being disturbed, hope at being rediscovered, exhaustion, hatred, depression. She was not used to such mental athletics, but now that her mind was active she found she was enjoying it. No matter what terrible truths were being disclosed to her, what terrifying facts she was learning, she was enjoying the experience.

'I think maybe we could talk for a long time,' she said to Damon. 'Now that I know my name, I think I can remember hearing it before. Not long ago.' She looked at Damon with what could almost have been a smile, had the nerves of her face been used to the act.

The two others in the room seemed disturbed by the increasingly familiar and normal conversation going on amongst them. One of them, an old man, stood and left with a series of nervous squeaks and grunts. The other one, a younger man, rested his hand gently on Pen's shoulder. 'Care,' he whispered, so quietly that even Damon did not hear him. Pen only nodded, and he too left.

'Now we are alone,' Pen said. She looked worried, twitched with a nervous energy where she sat on the damp floor.

'Yes.'

'So we can talk.'

'Yes.'

Though the intention had been stated, neither of the dispossessed said anything for five minutes. They sat in companionable silence, each with their own very different thoughts: Pen's new, frightened, like a child with adulthood instantly thrust upon it with no buffer of adolescence; Damon's ecstatic, revelling in the new-found life he felt, even smothering the worry that no matter how alive he did feel, the fact was that he had died years ago.

From elsewhere in the house came a thump, then silence again. Damon imagined a body rolling down the stairs, others watching impartially. He wanted to go to help, but how do you help a dead person? The paradox of his emotions struck him, the fact that he was thinking like a person alive, while all along he had been one of the many victims of Maélor. But unlike many he had not reached the final stage. True death would perhaps have been the best way, the natural way. But since it had been eluded, in however an unnatural way, Damon was determined to cling to what he had, and to build on it.

'What is Rick like?' Pen asked, ending the silence at last with a question that finally bridged the gap. Her stated interest in the outside, whatever was there, had finally woken her from her trance.

'He's fine,' Damon said, and then a scream interrupted his answer.

He had heard many screams in his life, and death. The worst were those in the basement under the Mesmer's house, the screams of the damned, the unconscious exhortations of the tortured. This scream was worse than all of them, more so because it undoubtedly came from one of the dispossessed downstairs. If a sound as terrible as that could come from a dead, emotionless thing, then whatever had caused it could only be one step away from the devil itself.

'What . . .?' Pen gasped.

Damon stood quickly, scanning the room as he did so. There was a window, if they needed it, but the drop would be at least ten feet, into darkness. If he could, he would prefer to leave the house the way he had come in.

'Stay here,' he whispered. The door had been pulled shut by the other two dispossessed as they left, and Damon pulled it open slowly, trying to anticipate the creaks and groans that would inevitably accompany its movement. As he did so another scream came from downstairs, this one louder and even more terrified than the first. He could not tell whether they had both come from the same person; they were sexless in their terror, indistinguishable in their blind panic.

Then, he heard the voice. 'What scares you?' it said.

Damon fell to his knees. If his heart had been beating, it would have stopped. If his mouth had been lubricated, it would have dried up. He felt a sensation in his back and balls, a cold, shivering impact that weighed down on him where he crouched in the rat shit and the accumulated waste of decades. His mind, so newly restored and cocky and proud in its new youth, seized up like a broken record player, grinding to a halt with a slurring realisation that he was doomed; doomed never to help Rick meet his missing girlfriend; doomed to feel the icy grasp of the Twin once more, view the terrible thing that Damon had seen in his hands; doomed, worst of all, to failure.

'What?' Pen hissed from across the room.

Damon turned slowly towards her, aware all the time of the presence of the ghoul on the floor below, trying not to imagine what he was doing down there, or what he was doing here. *Here to take you back, here to take us all back, the Mesmer doesn't like escapees.* Pen was sitting as he had left her, knees drawn up to her pale chin, arms clasped around her shins, hugging herself into the smallest shape possible.

'The . . . the . . .' Damon began, but he could not finish. How could he tell her so soon, only minutes after instilling her with a sense of hope, that damnation was downstairs to finish the job it had started? How could he really tell her that the Twin would be here soon, and that in a matter of hours, days at the most, the Mesmer would be at work again, bleeding the life and love from all of them, draining the very last dregs of humanity until the body simply let go?

Pen's eyes widened, taking in the pitiful sight of Damon scrabbling in the dirt at the door. She could still hear whimpers and distant screams. 'The Twin,' she stated.

Damon could only nod.

Another scream, this one cut off in mid-flow.

'We must go,' Pen said quietly, whispering automatically now that the danger was identified. The roles, she sensed, were in reverse. She was experiencing the release that Damon had been feeling for hours now, the new zest for existence, if not for life, that had been driving him since he had met Rick. But she guessed that in her, the feeling was stronger. Already there were memories. There was a park, and a presence that she loved. Sun, greenery, whispers of eternity. She was returning.

'Come on,' she hissed again, struggling to her feet.

Damon whimpered, then regained his composure when he saw what Pen was doing. The window was old, and rotted into the frame. She balled her fist and drove it through the glass, gashing her hand but drawing only a pathetic smear of blood. The broken glass sang on the concrete pavement outside, painfully loud in the silence of the building holding its breath.

Everything paused; Damon and Pen stood still, looking at each other with expressions that could have been comical in a different situation; the shouts from downstairs halted, and for a brief instant Damon wondered whether he had imagined them all in the first place, such was the silence in the house.

Then, from downstairs, another scream. This one was fury, not fear. There were no fears in the soul that issued that noise, only terror for those who heard it. Without speaking, it told of losses too great to bear, and warned of a future with no prospects except pain, and eventual, true death.

There was another scream and a thump, as of a body hitting a wall, and then hurried, heavy footsteps on the stairs.

Damon turned quickly to Pen. 'Go! Now, out the window, run!'

'Where . . .?' Pen muttered in desperation. She hardly knew who she was, let alone where she was or where she should go.

Damon hissed in frustration, heard the pounding footsteps coming nearer. How many stairs, he thought. Thirteen? Fifteen? He'd heard six, seven, eight . . .

'Just get out the window . . .'

. . . nine . . .

'. . . and run. We'll find each other.'

. . . ten . . .

'I've got to try to . . .'

'No!'

. . . eleven . . .

'No, he'll destroy you, you know what he has, you know his power.' Pen's expression held outright terror. This man had come to her and woken her from her death trance, only to throw himself in the path of the Twin. He would be utterly devastated, ruined beyond repair, given the true death in ways that no-one deserved. She could not, would not allow him to leave her now, not now.

. . . twelve . . .

'Pen, please!' Damon pleaded but he already knew it was too late. He could not persuade her to go in time, and in a few all too short moments, he would be facing the Twin once again. This time it would be as a dispossessed, perhaps with less to lose, but certainly with more knowledge of the consequences of loss. Even if the Twin did keep him to take back to the Mesmer, the prospects were little better than grim.

. . . thirteen . . .

The footsteps stopped at the top of the stairs. Damon froze, suddenly realising that the Twin did not know which room they were in. It was a big old house, there were perhaps six large rooms and three smaller bathrooms and storerooms on the first floor, all arranged around the central staircase and landing. Unless they made a noise, gave away their position, it would be potluck for the Twin. It gave them time, if only seconds, in which to escape.

Damon motioned for Pen to climb from the window. He grinned when he realised that this was one of the few moments when he was glad of not having to breathe, because holding his breath would have been a virtual impossibility with the fear of who was on the other side of the door. Pen stepped towards the window. A sliver of glass crushed itself under her foot, trying to dig into the bare floorboards.

A shout from outside.

In that brief instant, Damon decided what to do without really thinking about it. Indicating the window with his eyes, he turned and tugged the door open. He heard the crack of further glass behind him as Pen moved to the window, and in front of him came the charging form of the Twin. He kept his head down, not wanting to see the Twin's face as he ran towards the room, not wishing to see what he offered Damon in his outstretched hand, showing him his fears until they paralysed him. Instead, Damon shouted louder than he had in years, with feeling and passion, a shout that matched the enraged roar of the shape now only feet away from him on the landing.

Damon saw the shadow of Temple on the floor ahead of him, merging with his own cast out by the weak morning light. A second later they collided, Damon's head thumping into the Twin's midriff. He heard the monster's breath whoosh out of him, and grinned with satisfaction even as he felt his neck twisting awkwardly on his shoulders. He tumbled to the floorboards in a heap. He glanced at the Twin in time to see him stumbling backwards, hands buried in the flapping layers of clothing around his stomach, until he came to rest leaning against the landing balustrade.

Damon struggled to his knees, still trying to avoid catching the Twin's eye, knowing that if he did so the mesmeric qualities of the man's gaze could defeat him in seconds. Instead he kept his eyes on the Twin's feet, trying to gauge when he would make his move. Damon knew that by refusing to be drawn into the Twin's thoughts, he would be forcing physical attack. But this, he preferred.

He heard curses from the room he had just left, then a short scream brought to an abrupt halt. For a brief instant he thought the Twin had somehow eluded him, hypnotised him into thinking he was sitting in pain on the landing looking at the Twin's shoes, waiting for him to move, while all the time he was making his way to the room, catching Pen before she could make her escape. And then what? Torture, like before.

'You're not having her,' Damon hissed, and looked up.

The Twin smiled down at him. Damon realised the scream he had heard had probably been Pen falling from the window onto whatever lay below. It would not have hurt her badly, could not have, but if she had broken something she would be incapacitated for long enough for the Twin to catch her.

'My friends call me Temple,' the Twin said as he looked hungrily past Damon into the room.

'I'll bet you don't hear that name very often,' Damon replied, surprised and pleased at the defiant, taunting tone of his voice.

The Twin shrugged, but Damon could see the anger there beneath the sickening grin. 'No matter,' the huge man said. 'With friends like me, huh?' Damon's neck ached, he thought he may have cracked something in there. The pain was more a memory of pain, a dream of past injuries that had dislocated or broken, but it was enough to cause him discomfort. He twisted his head to look into the room behind him, and heard a grating like crushed glass within his neck. When he turned back, he was looking at the Twin's outstretched hand, the glittering haze of promise which swathed it in silky streamers, twisting and turning as he slowly moved his hand up and down, left and right.

'What scares you? What terrifies you, what make you sit and stare for weeks at the places you once frequented? What make you mourn your life, dispossessed? What makes you squirm, dispossessed?' Temple stepped slowly towards the shattered shape on the floor, feeling no threat from the sad remnant but always careful, always aware that even pitiful dispossessed like this one sometimes had surprises up their sleeves.

The escape, for instance. Years ago, but still remembered.

The open door of the room taunted him, encouraged him on with the promise of his goal within. For surely the girl, Summers, was in there? She was a wreck, almost one of those that the dispossessed insisted on calling lessers, the lowest of the low. Surely she could not find it within herself to try to escape?

Damon realised his mistake, but his anger was swallowed in an all-consuming fear of what he saw before him. For most dispossessed it was the same, the image they saw in the hand of the Twin, if he ever had cause to let them see it.

The Mesmer, Maélor, hovering above Temple's hand, life-size and yet still contained in the palm of the man who had come to kill him. His face was grim, amused, as he had so often looked before torturing and bleeding one of his victims of life. He felt such hatred coming from that shape, a wave of overwhelming malice directed specifically at him, that it almost froze the intimidating presence of the Twin from his mind, a blind spot in his imagination. The fear drove him to the floor, rising within him like some long lost emotion, shaking off the ashes of its resurrection to squeeze his still heart with its bloody fingers.

Temple smiled with satisfaction at the squirming shape before him, then stepped towards the room. 'You were so nearly back as well, it seems,' Temple commented as he passed Damon.

The words cut through Damon's fear, phrases he thought should mean something, but which were encoded by the mist of his terror. A shadow passed before him, behind the images of his fears imprinted on his retina, and stepped over his outstretched, twitching legs.

Fear of failure.

The wall of faces, tortured souls displaying their displacement in stone for the pleasure of their killers.

Fear of betrayal.

The image of Maélor faded from his eyes, and Damon looked up, startled. The Twin was stepping over him, his long coat wafting in the breeze caused by his movement. His left foot passed over Damon's now still legs, laces flapping. Damon wondered which corpse he had stolen those boots from.

He reached out suddenly, grabbing the Twin's left leg at the ankle, twisting with all his might and pushing at the same time. The weight of Temple's body twisting and falling pulled Damon from his sitting position. He went with the flow and came to his feet, falling forwards onto the sprawling figure of the Twin, releasing his ankle and driving his fists into his side, his back, his neck, again and again.

Temple let out a surprised grunt, and for precious seconds the shock made him unable to regain his thoughts and protect himself. He felt the ineffectual thumps from the dispossessed on top of him raining down on his back, but it was not these he was concerned about. What did concern him was the brief view he had gained into the room before he had been brought down. The bare room was empty of anything: no furniture, no carpet, no Penny Summers. The window was smashed and open to the elements. She had gone. He struggled to his feet with the bothersome remnant still struggling on his back.

Damon realised that he would not be able to hold the Twin, let alone fight him. Temple would drag him into the room with him, drag him through the window if necessary, and at best he was only a cumbersome burden to the monster. Certainly not a threat, or an opponent. Damon acted rapidly, the process of thought quicker than that of understanding, and he tugged the Twin once, hard, using the weight of his own tilting body to pull the huge shape after him. The banister hit Damon's back, creaked for an agonising second, then snapped under the combined weight of the two men. In a shower of sawdust and grunts they fell, Damon still holding on tightly, and crashed down into the hallway.

Wood splintered under the impact, and Damon was readying himself to fall further, into the cellar below. But the floor held firm, dust swirling in an angry cloud, settling on the new deformed shapes in its midst.

Damon had landed on top of the Twin, who seemed to have been dazed by the impact. He tried to get off, but found his left arm trapped under the great weight of the man, his wrist pierced in several places by the splintered floorboards. He was preparing himself to rip his arm free when the Twin opened his eyes. Damon averted his gaze, but the big man was far too angry to attempt his hypnosis.

Temple was furious. He sensed his position at once, and an inner satisfaction gleamed visibly on the skin of his right hand. He shouted in the face of his aggressor, sat upright, gripped the remnant's shattered arm that was somehow stuck in the floor below him. He threw him off like a bag of feathers, pleased with the sound his body made when it hit the damp wall. He stood, walked to the tattered mess who had so bravely and foolishly taken him on. Temple felt a brief flash of respect for the shape before him, but then disgust wiped it away with a dismissive hand.

'Die,' Temple said. He grabbed hold of Damon's left leg. His hand glowed brighter, the silvery shine trickling over into Damon's flesh, bringing from him a staccato scream. The pain was too much to cry properly. 'Die,' Temple repeated. He squeezed tighter.

A minute later the Twin was standing in front of the house. He sensed dispossessed all around, watching him from the shadows like the vermin they were, waiting for him to go so that they could scatter and hide again. Well, he would let them. All but one. And he was sure she would not have gone far before going to ground.

fourteen

Pen was as still and as quiet as a tree. Anyone who saw her, anyone *Normal*, would have known that she was a corpse. There was no movement to her body at all; no twitching limbs, no rise and fall of her chest as she drew breath, no rhythmic jumping of a pulse on her neck or wrist. Her eyes were glazed and dry and staring at the moss-covered facade of an old stone wall, seeing nothing. Her hair shifted slightly with an occasional breeze that nosed along the side of the building; other than that, all was still.

A seed of doubt, and hope, and curiosity had been planted in her tired mind by the short conversation she had just had with Damon. But as yet, the seed was buried deep, beyond the reach of random musings, taking root and spreading its base before it reared its head again and told her that there was more than this. The action she had just taken — the flight from the room, the long drop to the damp ground below, the several minutes of running and scrambling through back gardens and side streets and silent roads — was the most significant of the last few years. She had felt something within her as she ran, something apart from the dim sense of everything being terribly wrong: life. She had felt invigorated, vaulting over rotten garden fences to escape the evil man chasing her. The man who was looking to do to her again what he had done years before. Her actions came as near to the real world, real existence, as any she had taken since her escape from the Mesmer all those years ago, and her subsequent flight into purgatory.

But now, with the excitement over, the memory of Damon was already growing faint and indistinct in her mind, the words he had said lost, to be found again only when the seed he had planted took root.

Pen turned her head slightly at the sound of a bird fluttering in the tree above her. A spider, startled by the sudden movement from the surface beneath it, scurried down her neck and arm and hid away in the fold of her jeans where her knee was bent. Its web was forgotten for now, its initial bracings still evident on Pen's head and shoulders. Pen's eyes moved in their sockets, moistening again, the soreness caused by not blinking hardly bothering her at all. The sound of the bird came again and Pen looked up into the tree. It was still too dark to see anything, although morning was approaching rapidly from the east.

As Pen sat beneath the tree, light slowly filtered through the bushes and shrubs and splayed itself on the wall next to her, the advance party of morning establishing territory over night. Her pupils contracted slowly as the light increased. Moisture on her face and hair began to dry imperceptibly. Her knee joint creaked as she moved, and the spider fled the proposed web site altogether and rattled away into the undergrowth to give a fly a bad day.

Rick was your boyfriend, before the Mesmer took us.

The words appeared in Pen's mind as if from nowhere, and she looked around in confusion. Standing, peering cautiously between the bushes and out onto the road they bordered, Pen waited for the words again. They had seemed to spark something in her, a feeling of dread that the name Mesmer inspired, and a feeling that she was sure she had felt for years and years, but only now acknowledged. The name grated on her mind like a ragged metal splinter, piercing areas here and there that were memory, hate and terror, encouraging her to explore the name further. She did not sense the memory appearing, but was soon aware of a picture in her mind. The content drove her to her knees, the knowledge of what was happening in the picture and the certainty of who it was happening to was too much for her. As she remembered the Mesmer's distorted groin plunging at her face she shook her head and shouted in denial.

Birds took flight above her and she decided that it was time to do the same. But where to go? She found that she was without a destination, a circumstance that she had not been in for such a long time. Before today, randomness was her ruler, her guide and her life, and destinations were wherever she ended up. Now there was something else. First of all, the relevance of what had happened that night and the fact that she could still remember vague parts of it. Secondly, the fear she still felt, a fear that someone or something was looking for her, something that it would be very foolish to let catch her. Finally, the memory she had just experienced of the Mesmer doing those things to her, bleeding her of her life and love and hope, and of the face she had seen briefly behind the Mesmer before pain blocked the view. The face of Damon.

Pen tried to remember. She walked, choosing the left, feeling that it was the correct way because it was into the light. And as she went, she opened her mind and began to search it.

'What scares you, then, sweetie?'

Pen halted in her tracks. She looked up and saw Temple standing before her, the Twin in all his ambiguous glory, face smiling and frowning, eyes wide with excitement, and narrow with a calculating evil.

He held his hand out to her, opened it.

Pen screamed. Dancing in front of her, sprouting from the hand of the Twin, was the Twin. Pen felt new emotions only recently rediscovered shrivelling in the face of the double terror before her. The memories of Damon and the tenuous thoughts of Rick flew away into the conflagration of terror within her, and her mind cleared itself of everything except that which she now faced.

The Twin. Temple. Sadistic, cruel, enjoying the tortures that he had inflicted upon her so many years ago and now enjoying them again in retrospect. Pen felt every blow from the cellar eight years before, every slimy tongue trail drawn upon her by this monster, every bruise he left her with as he went for the night, only to return again in the morning. And now here he was again, twice as terrifying, twice as dreadful in the promise her memories held for him, and for her.

Temple looked to his side and laughed as he saw what was displayed there on his hand. The Summer girl's fears, those deeply embedded terrors that he was even now drawing upon, were of him. Smug, complimented by her panic, Temple reached out to hold her. The image in his palm dissipated like mist in a storm as he grabbed her, but still she stood like a mannequin, unable to move, unable to think, only remembering and dreading what future there remained.

Temple hoisted her over his shoulder and heard a small whimper from her shocked body. 'Alright, sweet,' he said, still pleased with what he had just seen. To be someone's ultimate terror, even if that someone had been effectively dead for nearly a decade . . . was gratifying.

It gave him encouragement to do what he was about to do.

'Let's go see the Mesmer,' Temple whispered with contempt. 'See if his old magic really has left him.'

*   *   *

Liz went to work, Rick stayed at home, feigning illness. He phoned in to his office and complained of a stomach bug, feeling only a brief burst of guilt.

He wandered the house for a few vacant minutes, looking for something to do, needing to occupy his time with thoughts other than the bitter memory of yesterday's unfinished conversation. He walked across the landing, felt a tug as something attracted his gaze upwards, to the loft hatch.

He pulled down the loft access ladder and climbed, excitement growing within him every second.

The boxes were still where he had stacked them years before. Luckily the loft was dry and well ventilated, so only the top couple of books in each box were curled and yellowed with damp. Rick sat in the boarded attic and smiled as he brought out the books.

It was like taking his past from a cupboard. With each book he brought out, associated memories leapt at him like unhindered genies. Memories not only of the book and the story it contained, but sometimes of where he was reading it, with whom, when. The smells of the cooking as he read *The War of the Worlds* over a bubbling curry. The soporific swaying of a train carriage as he revelled in the space opera of *Consider Phlebas*.

The warm body next to him in bed, the sweet smells of recent sex hanging in the air, Pen's beautiful black hair draped across her pillow as he settled into a story of talking animals and Spellsinging.

Before he knew it Rick was sitting within a fortress of books. They rose around him on all sides in untidy piles, some collapsed and splayed on the floor like oversized packs of cards. The loft rang with the gentle hum of nostalgia, and even though many of the memories were happy and Rick was grateful to have them, he did wonder why most recollections held a taste of sadness.

Before he could reach for a fourth box, Rick saw the book he knew he wanted to read. Pen had loved it. He grabbed it and made his way down the loft ladder, forgetting to box the other books.

He decided to go out for a walk, find a quiet bench in the park, immerse himself once again into the sad, uncertain world of Rick Deckard.

With the novel tucked into his jacket pocket, Rick left the house.

fifteen

One of the overriding images of Rick's childhood was of a dead dog, victim of the roads. He and a friend had found it where it had crawled to die, lying bleeding and panting under a bush on a roundabout. As they approached it the animal began to whine and whimper, and made vain attempts to growl at them. Rick felt that the creature wanted them to leave, and in truth he had been scared of facing death in the face. Until that moment, death was what happened to the bad guys in *The Sweeney*, or the shouting Germans in the war films when Clint Eastwood or John Wayne blew them away. Death was not lying under a bush with no-one taking care of you, breathing in the fumes of your own innards as they slowly seeped from your shattered body; it was not the smell he had sensed as they ran onto the roundabout, the sickly mixture of shit and puke and decay already setting in; in short, death was not here, was not now.

But they were children, and they had gone to the dog.

The noises he heard as he approached his house later that afternoon reminded him of the dying mongrel so many years ago. The whimpers and sobs were beyond pleading, resigned rather than desperate. The shivering form he saw huddled on his doorstep looked like an animal at first, and the pungent odour that assailed his nostrils as he walked past the broken front gate seemed to confirm this impression. But as he drew nearer the sounds changed. The voice shocked him.

'Rick . . . he's got her . . .'

Rick ran to the front door. The wreck on his doorstep was Damon. The smell came from the gangrenous mess of his leg. His face was drawn, grey, the image of a Romero zombie, only worse. Real. His eyes held little hope. They were as dark as the eternal night they craved.

'Rick,' Damon whispered once more, 'he's got her. The Twin. Pen. Took her.'

Rick bent down, ignoring the mess and the smell. He ran his hand over Damon's face and was surprised at how cold he felt. Damon grabbed his wrist, held it.

'We must help her. I know where he's taking her, I know where to go, we must . . . oh God, to go there again! I don't think I can, not on my own.'

'You're not going anywhere like this,' Rick said. 'Come on, inside.' He leaned down to lift Damon and drag him against the front door while he opened it. Mr Rational asked him what he was doing, dragging a dying dead man into his house hours before Liz was going to return home from work. Rick told Mr Rational to get stuffed.

The door opened and Damon fell across the threshold with a groan. Rick dragged him inside, thought briefly about an ambulance then decided the questions may be a little awkward. How to explain you need help for a man who says he's already died once before.

'Shall I get you a drink or . . .'

'No, No! No time, for God's sake.' Damon struggled into a sitting position in the hallway, pulling himself up and bracing himself against the wall.

'What happened?' Rick asked.

'No time for that. We must go, you must come with me.'

Rick mused on this for a moment, considering how preposterous he would have considered this situation only a couple of days ago. 'First, tell me what happened,' he said.

Damon screwed his face into a rictus of pain and frustration, shook his head. 'No time . . .'

'You don't tell me, I don't go,' Rick said firmly. 'I throw you out. No skin off my nose, you're dead anyway.' He said the last few words without conviction, realised that Damon would not believe him.

'When I left you,' Damon said, 'I went to the calling.'

He told Rick what had happened in Cheltenham, skipping the irrelevant details, concentrating more on the conversation he had begun with Pen in the hope that talk of her might persuade Rick to go with him.

When he had finished, Rick was quiet for some time, staring at the ceiling, almost immobile where he leant against the wall across from Damon. 'She remembered me?' he asked quietly.

'Yes.'

'How is she?'

Damon almost smiled. Almost. Rick uttered a humourless laugh.

'But it can be made worse for her,' Damon said. 'The Mesmer can make it much, much worse. If the Twin gets her there before us, he can put her through more than . . . more than you can possibly imagine.' He rested his head against the cold wall, exhausted.

'He's not a character I'm particularly keen to meet. Maybe we should call the police.'

Damon said nothing. It was enough to let Rick think this through for himself and disregard it with another snort.

'Yeah, right. What an idiot! Who's going to believe . . .? Hell, I don't really believe.' Rick looked down at the man in his hallway who professed to being dead. 'How did you get here?'

'Hitched.'

'Your leg smells.'

'I rode in the back.'

'It figures,' Rick smiled. He looked at Damon's leg, the sticky mess of his jeans that hid the ruin beneath. 'He did that just by touching you?'

Damon nodded tiredly.

There were a few minutes of silence, punctuated only by Rick walking slowly to the kitchen and pouring a glass of water. He handed it to Damon back in the hallway, who drank the useless fluid out of politeness. The pain was still there. It would not go.

Rick looked at him. He saw what most people would take for a madman. He saw someone who Liz would shrink from in the street. He saw a character who had come into his life in the last couple of days and turned it upside down; his wife becoming distant and upset, he himself being encouraged to drive a hundred miles with some notion that a girl who had died eight years ago was stumbling around somewhere, waiting for him to rescue her like some supernatural knight. He saw someone who hurt, not only from the pain of his leg, if he actually felt pain, but from memories too terrible to even try to comprehend. Memories of torture, if he was to be believed, and eventual, awful death.

Liz was mad at him. She had not talked to him for nearly a day. It could hardly get much worse.

'Alright,' Rick said. 'I'll go. Where?'

'Cornwall,' Damon whispered.

What the hell will Liz think? Mr Rational asked, but Rick ignored him once more. He would leave a note for her, telling her that he would be back tomorrow, that he was going to settle the whole thing today, tonight, in one go.

Make things right.

However much he really believed any of this, Rick decided that it was worth one more trip.

'We'll go now,' he said.

sixteen

The girl sat silently in the back of the car, barely moving, her eyes lowered and squeezed half shut for most of the ride. She was slight, a faded impression of what she had been while alive, pale, decidedly unattractive. Temple knew she had been pretty in her time.

He was glad the girl was quiet. It was a long drive, tiring, the spectacular views towards the end of the journey doing nothing to alleviate the weariness that Temple felt by the time they reached the moors. The Summer girl seemed not to notice her surroundings. She could have screamed all the way down here, he knew, with the memories he had awoken within her and the promise of more of the same experiences to come. But she had withdrawn into herself. He had only dealt with dead ones a couple of times before, when he could catch them. They were usually quiet like this, but became agitated when they reached the moor.

'Nearly there,' he said, and grunted in satisfaction as the girl's eyes opened. She raised her head. He saw a semblance of life return to her face, a twisted expression of dawning fear. 'Not long now,' he added, enjoying the reaction his words stirred in her. She began to mumble.

Dawn felt its way tentatively across the moors, drawing a soft mist from the sodden ground. Temple relaxed back in his seat and let the sleepiness wash over him again as he began to recognise twists in the road, rocks huddled like sleeping dinosaurs in the heather. Pen continued to whimper behind him until he raised his hand, fist closed, in plain view. She was silenced immediately. He laughed.

Ten minutes later he saw the house looming out of the mist. It was old but pleasant looking, the stone walls bounding the property tumbled into a vague impression of their ancient glory, windows speckled with cracked paint. The plants in the garden had blossomed only recently; wild flowers, heathers, roses, even some orchids which Maélor had planted at one time in the past and which had somehow managed to survive.

Temple giggled to himself, a low, gruff growl which made Pen moan in the back seat, try to reach for the door handle for the first time during their journey. He reached round and slapped her hand back into her lap. She glanced at him, then lowered her eyes again.

Pen's mind was in the past, ignoring the eight years of lonely existence she had strolled through, forgetting even her death and reawakening into something worse. She only recalled the tortures. The pain inflicted upon her by the Twin, and even worse, the terrible feeling of her whole life draining into the Mesmer's mutated crotch. The myriad faces of those who had been here before where they twisted and rolled in the wall of souls, their expressions describing torments beyond even her meagre imaginings. She twitched in her seat as the door next to her was tugged open and a cold draught puffed mist into the car.

'Come on, let's go and see who's home,' the Twin murmured.

He dragged her through the break in the old wall that marked the ambiguous entrance to the garden. As he neared the house he realised how much it had deteriorated in the year he had been away. The gutter hung from one fixing, moisture collected from the morning dew dripping steadily down the wall of the house, following a dark patch where more water before it had left its mark. The windows were not only in need of decoration, they were rotting from the outside in. The downstairs windows showed signs of tampering; chunks of wood stuck from the softened timber like broken teeth, as if someone or something had been trying to force their way in.

He wondered whether Maélor was even still here.

As if in answer to the unspoken thought, the front door swung open. Maélor stood in the dark rectangle formed by the door. He looked at Temple and Pen without expression, as if he had known they would be here. His face was emotionless.

'Hello, Temple,' he said.

Pen screamed and was instantly silenced by Temple. He held her face, a brief spark lit his hand and she dropped to the damp ground. He turned to look at Maélor, his old master, the thing he had come here to confront, fight if necessary, and defeat. Maélor was a Mesmer, a black wizard, a twister of minds and an eater of souls. Looking at him, shrunken and wilted and old and wrinkled, Temple smiled with utter confidence. He would win. No doubt.

'You've changed,' he said. 'You've got old.'

Maélor shrugged. 'I've not fed for a while. I'll not feed again. I've had enough, and now I'll wait to see what happens. And when. Why did you bring the girl, Temple?'

Temple glanced casually down at Pen as if he had forgotten she was there. 'Gift for you,' he said.

Maélor stared at Pen for a long, quiet moment. Temple could not read the look in his eyes, the expression on his face, for there was none. Maélor may as well have been dead for all the signs of life he displayed in his actions or movements.

The Mesmer looked back at Temple. 'I told you on the telephone, Temple. I've finished.' He nodded at Pen. 'I've no need of her any more. Get rid of her.' He turned to go back into the house.

Temple stepped after him, reached out a hand, hesitated.

Maélor paused without turning around. 'Raise your hand to me, Temple?' he said quietly.

Temple felt the first squirms of doubt, but quickly dispelled them with images of Maélor beneath his feet, trampled, dead. 'You're lost,' he said angrily.

Maélor looked back briefly. 'Finished, maybe. But still powerful.' He opened his eyes fractionally wider and for a brief instant Temple felt the full, staggering force of his mesmeric powers. Then he disappeared into the house.

The Twin staggered, stumbling back and almost tripping over Pen's prone form. He shook his head to clear the fogginess and thought about stepping after Maélor, taking him on in the house. Then he thought of something better. In the dark of the hallway he could just see the entrance door to the cellar, innocuously standing sentinel to the understair space, hiding horrors worse than any normal person usually faces in a lifetime.

'Wake up, Summers.' He nudged Pen with his foot. She stirred but remained unconscious. He kicked her, harder this time, and she was startled awake, eyes wide and blank. He leaned down and grabbed her hair before she could get her bearings and dragged her into the house.

She screamed once, an involuntary sound, but then her throat constricted with the terror of where she was, who she was with, who she was near. She could almost smell the Mesmer, sensing him in every room, surrounding her with his presence.

Temple reached the door and yanked it open, drawing in the foul air of the basement with a pleasant sense of *déjŕ vu*. He revelled in the recollections, smiling in spite of his stress, until he heard Maélor's voice again.

'I don't go down there any more,' the Mesmer said from across the hallway. He looked small in his old suit, ancient, weak and vulnerable. Temple knew he was anything but these, but still the impression lingered.

Temple faced him. 'Why not, old man? Why are you scared of yourself? You know you need what you do down here . . .'

'Did . . .'

Temple paused. 'Did. That's right.' Without turning to look he flung Pen into the shadows. She screamed as she tumbled down the old stone stairs into a darkness more profound than death.

Temple smiled at Maélor. 'I will go, if you're scared.'

'I can't let you do that,' Maélor said.

Temple stood taller, prouder, sensing that he was overplaying the threat from his old master. He was now the shrunken image of a man who had once commanded undying respect and devotion; nothing more than an empty, vacuous joke. 'Stop me,' he challenged.

The front door, which had drifted shut on its hinges after Temple had dragged Pen inside, swung open. It struck the stone wall inside and puffed up a cloud of dust.

The Twin spun round, an angry grimace turning his face into a smile, and a frown. 'Who the fuck are you?' he hissed.

'I've brought an old friend to see you,' Rick said, and stepped aside so that Damon could join him in the hallway.

For a brief moment, over too soon, the four stood in the hallway of the dilapidated house like a waxwork scenario. Then Damon slumped against the doorjamb as his wounded leg gave way once again. He was groaning.

Rick heard complete surrender in the sound. He wondered how the two characters in front of him could inspire such hopelessness in another human being, but then he remembered that Damon could not strictly be categorised as that any more. He was dead, so he said. Killed with Pen.

Pen.

'Where's Penny?' Rick asked quietly. He recognised the Twin from Damon's description of him, the tall one by the stairs with the face that may have been smiling, but still held threat and anger within its features.

Maélor did not move, simply stared. Temple edged forward, then halted as if changing his mind.

'Where is she?' Rick asked again, more forcefully.

'Dead,' Maélor said quietly. 'Dead many years ago now.'

Rick stared at him, feeling a dizziness as he met the Mesmer's eyes and looking down quickly at the man's collar. 'And you killed her,' he hissed.

Maélor nodded soberly. 'Yes, that's right.'

Rick noticed an almost imperceptible glance from Temple into the doorway behind him, and realised that Pen was in the basement. He remembered Damon's description of the terrible underground room, with the wall of souls and the ghosts of hundreds mourning their agony. He looked down at where Damon lay sprawled at his feet, his leg steadily seeping through his trousers, eyes shut, forehead furrowed as he rocked back and forth in his despair.

All true. Everything he told me, true.

'It's all true?' he asked.

Maélor nodded. 'It used to be. Now, no more. Now, I'm dying a normal death.'

'You fucking idiot!' Temple roared, obviously itching to launch himself at someone, his feet stamping at the ground like an enraged bull.

Maélor glanced at the Twin then looked back at Rick. 'I'll end your friend for you. And the woman.'

'End them?' Rick frowned, but he already guessed what he meant.

'Put them at rest,' Maélor nodded.

'Fool!' Temple said, his voice pitched high with emotion. 'You're giving up everything! You're going to die a normal death, useless, fucking scum! Useless!' He began to laugh as he said it, because all he could imagine was himself in the cellar, adding the face of the old Mesmer to the wall of souls.

His wall of souls.

Maélor stood his ground against Temple's verbal onslaught, hardly moving, the expression on his face sad, wistful, but still hard and uncompromising. 'Remember what I said? Remember, on the phone only days ago?

> "Greater is the man who, in the shadow of death,
>> Revels in the victories of his years,
>> Dwells upon the triumphs of his tears,
>> Smiles at his end, content in fate."'

There was silence for a few moments while the words sunk in to all those present. Temple scoffed, spat onto the old carpet, laughed. 'Old goat!'

'I've no triumphs to revel in,' Maélor said. 'I was made to do what I did, I was born to kill and hurt, but I achieved nothing. I can revel in only one achievement: that of ending what I have done. That is why I smile at my end. That is why I am content. But you, Temple, have dreams and ambitions that I cannot allow.'

'Then smile while I end you,' Temple said, and he opened his hand. 'What scares you, loser?'

Rick gasped at what he saw. On Temple's hand, and sheathed around it in wisps of a sickly grey light, stood an image of the Mesmer. It was a different Maélor to the one who stood aghast before him now. This one seemed taller, his face dark and grimacing, his body naked and gaunt, eyes full of an impenetrable darkness that held only a promise of pain. His crotch was deformed in a terrible way; the only growth that resembled a penis twisted and turned in the air before him like a snake dancing to the music of death. His hands reached out and grasped the air as if he could torture even that.

Maélor stumbled back to the tune of Temple's laughter, but then the atmosphere changed instantly. The Mesmer composed himself and smiled through the fear; the fear of continuing as he was; the terror he felt at the murders he had fed himself with, the people he had condemned to an immortality of pain and torment. He looked at the terrible vision to Temple's right and drew strength from it, feeding from his own mortal fears as he had fed for so long on the minds and souls of so many others.

Temple staggered back as he saw what he held. He realised the implication of the vision only too well, and the smile on Maélor's face only confirmed his fears. His eyes were drawn to Maélor's where they grew dark and wide in his horribly smiling face.

Maélor looked from the vision of his old self — the self he now knew he had defeated — and he used the full force of his life-long powers as Temple met his gaze.

The Twin fell backwards as if hit by a sudden wind, his arms pin-wheeling, legs striking up and out as his feet tangled. His hand closed and the image vanished into the dank air, flickering around his hand and the ceiling of the hallway like St Elmo's fire. He hit the floor on his back, half in and half out of the opening to the basement. He grunted into the sudden silence as he struggled to gain purchase, but his co-ordination had been knocked from him and he tumbled out of sight into the dark.

Rick stared wide-eyed at the old man before him, who now stooped and grasped his chest, panting. He took a step towards him, but Damon's voice held him.

'Don't! He'll take you, he'll do to you what he did to me.' Damon struggled into a sitting position against the open front door, eyes pleading, the terror he so obviously felt at being in this place still more than apparent in his eyes.

Maélor looked at Rick, but seemed too tired to speak. Rick saw the truth in his eyes, the honesty of his intentions. The Mesmer stepped towards the basement stairs and without further ado disappeared into the dark.

Rick knelt at Damon's side. 'Damon. He said he'd end you. Give you peace.'

Damon shook his head, groaning in frustration. 'He lies. His existence . . . is a lie to life. He's unnatural . . . yet he's here. He lies, Rick. God help us, and Pen.'

Rick suddenly wanted to see Pen, to see her more than anything. He thought he believed in what the Mesmer had said. But before the old man did whatever he had to do to Pen to let her rest in peace . . . he had to see her.

'I'll come back for you in a minute,' Rick said. Then he stood and stepped cautiously towards the open basement doorway.

seventeen

Rick was half way down the worn staircase when the scream stopped him cold. His spine tingled, his balls shivered as if an ice-cold breeze had breathed up from the darkness below. It was like the frenzied squeal of a trapped fox as the hounds close for the kill, or the inhuman shout of a mother witnessing her child's murder. He sat down hard on one of the cold stone steps.

'Jesus Christ!' The scream still echoed, whether from the old walls or simply in his mind he could not tell. He heard faint groanings from behind him, the sound having disturbed Damon where he lay in pain in the hallway above. He stared down into the darkness, trying to discern shapes in the dim light that seemed to suffuse the chamber. He saw only a wall at the bottom of the stairs, dull grey, damp rock covered with a slimy growth of mould.

His heart still jumping with the shock of the scream, Rick started down the stairs again. Six more to go, five, four . . .

He heard another sound from the room below, much quieter than the scream but equally as shocking in what it implied. It was a tearing, like wet fabric being ripped, ending with a crack like wood on stone.

Then, a splash.

Dripping. A thud.

He rounded the corner.

A huge inrush of terrible images hit Rick all at once, and instantly his mind insulated him from what he was witnessing and drove the images distant, like events viewed through a reversed telescope.

Maélor stood in the centre of the room, hands raised to shoulder height on either side of his body, blood and a thick lumpy mess dripping steadily from his hands onto the huddled shape at his feet . . .

. . . the huddled shape at his feet, the shape of Temple, now seemingly shrunken and malformed, blood pooling rapidly around the hole where his guts should be, the grey mess of his intestines a steaming pile several feet from his body . . .

. . . several feet from his body at the base of a wall. The wall of souls. A wall that heaved and squirmed with the faces of those who had lost themselves in this basement. The pained images came and went as he watched, as if pushed out from behind. They started as discolourations in the stone surface, rapidly changing into definite faces with dark, sorrowful expressions. A spider ran from floor to ceiling, seemingly unperturbed by the strange eruptions taking place beneath its scampering legs. It passed over the mouth of a screaming woman as the wall smoothed again, and soon it was in the eye of an old man, then the hair of a child . . .

Pen, in the corner. She stared at Rick with a smile on her face, a dreamy gaze that he remembered from many years ago, the smile he had fallen in love with, the gap between her front teeth . . .

'Pen . . .' Rick muttered, but Maélor stepped in front of him. 'That is not your girl,' he said.

Rick began to cry, the impact of all he had seen not yet reaching him, but the simple realisation that he was in the same room as his old girlfriend drawing the tears from him. 'Pen?' he cried.

The girl stood unsteadily and began to walk to him. She skirted the bloody mess in the middle of the basement, stopping to stare at the dead face below her. In death, the Twin looked as fearful as when he had been alive. His grey face had eyes open, yet closed. The ambiguity of his appearance was gradually fading as steam slowed from his open stomach. Soon, maybe, he would look normal.

Pen stepped past Temple and approached Rick where he stood backed against the wall. 'Rick?'

Maélor reached out before Rick had a chance to touch the girl. He closed his hand over her face and frowned, concentrating. She sighed once and collapsed onto the floor in a heap.

Rick thought he saw a shimmer in the wall, an increased flow of its trapped souls, but he may have been wrong. He thought that maybe he should feel angry with Maélor, but as he looked into the Mesmer's eyes he realised that all he had to do was leave.

Leave

Leave and let

Leave and let the Mesmer

Leave and let the Mesmer do his work. Finish everything.

He turned and left.

Damon sat in the front doorway, his moaning now silenced. He still moved slightly, but did not notice when Rick approached him. Rick thought he should stay and help him, bend down and make sure his leg was all right. But then something gave him a mental shove in the back, and as soon as he was through the door he forgot about Damon.

He did not look back at the house as he approached his car. He fumbled for his keys in his jacket pocket, but then remembered that he had put them in his jeans. He started the car. As he drove away he was aware of nothing behind him. No house. No tumbled down wall. No body, sprawled in a doorway. No memories. Nothing.

epilogue

She stared at him from the polished oak desk. The photo was from before the craziness of the spring. Her eyes in the picture were carefree and cheeky, not haunted and older looking as they were now. Her hair was the same; short, shining with vitality and health, although now she had plans to grow it long.

Rick looked at the picture of his wife and felt a deep, warm satisfaction in his chest. It was the kind of feeling he could never describe to anyone adequately, a love that held her with him when they were apart. He smiled as he remembered her cheeky laugh, feeling for a moment that she was there in the room. He was looking forward to going home tonight.

They were going to go and fetch a video, cuddle up on the settee with a bottle of wine, maybe an Indian take-away later, then bed. Try again to make a baby. Rick had never experienced anything so erotic as making love with the specific aim to make a child.

He sat back and sighed, trying to wrap himself with the contentment he felt, but at the same time finding it impossible to dismiss the nagging doubts in the back of his mind. They reared their heads at the most inconvenient of times, the latest being the meeting he had had with his boss that morning. They had been discussing new accounts, fee scales for future contracts, then Rick could think only of a loud scream, wet dripping sounds, Pen walking towards him with a smile on her face.

He had excused himself, splashed water over his face in the toilets, blamed the strange spell on the residue of the glandular fever he had suffered from in the early summer. He'd been run down, the doctor had said. Prone to infection, not surprising he had caught something nasty like this.

The cloud was still there within him, demanding his attention, and whether he liked it or not he would have to face it some time. He had spoken with dead people and seen a murder, returned home in a daze and been unable to explain anything to Liz when she challenged him. Since then, her anger had subsided as she watched him suffer, really suffer, with the memories he carried within him. She had successfully diverted her own attention from the truth, or not, of what had happened to him by concentrating on his well-being, and the time soon came when she was better than him. She had helped him through the worst of his times, seeing the loss but hardly understanding what it meant.

Rick tapped his pen on the desktop, humming tunelessly to himself, a tune that he would never remember again.

He glanced at the paperback on his desk, the bookmark an hour from the end. It was *Do Androids Dream of Electric Sheep*. Rick Deckard had been searching for something as well; something lost, something hidden. Beyond his reach.

Rick had read dozens of books since the spring, eagerly wading into the infinite well of dreams and possibilities they barely tapped. This book, however, remained unfinished. The bookmark preserved the place he had stopped at before finding the dying man on his doorstep. He meant to finish it, he really did, but he felt that opening it would only continue something that, he hoped, was over.

He stared from the window at the blazing heat of one of the hottest summers on record. The park he could see from his office was brown and dead through lack of water, yet it was still attractive to the devoted sun worshippers, much to the delight of the other members of the office. Lunchtime was like a trip to the zoo.

He was remembering the house more and more, and as the memories returned so did the need to return there himself, to see what was left, to come to terms with what Maélor had done and, hopefully, understand it. There was never any doubt in his mind as to the intentions of the Mesmer. Impossible to put things right, but Rick was sure he wanted at the very least to put an end to the suffering he had caused. But still, thoughts of Pen and Damon lingered. He knew he would have to go back . . . he had to see.

That evening he told Liz what he was thinking. She was unhappy, but seemed almost keen for him to travel back down to Cornwall. Perhaps to exorcise his own thoughts, any guilt he had. Perhaps to clear his mind. Give her back her old husband. Make him well.

*   *   *

He drove unerringly, straight to the house. The sun was still there, burning the heather and scarring the moorlands brown and grey, sucking moisture from the ground and drifting thin mists over the cracked earth. The house itself had no life surrounding it at all. When Rick parked the car and stepped into the heat, sweat immediately sticking his shirt to his back and running down his sides, he noticed only the colours of decay; brown heather, ochre grasses where they still stood, fragile and waiting for a breeze to break their stems, and the greyness of the house. The walls surrounding it seemed even more demolished than before, barely more than piles of stones now, hardly recognisable at all as a man-made structure.

He wiped his brow, trying to blame his increased heartbeat on the heat. He was not afraid, as such — he could see and sense that there was nothing alive here, nor anything undead, simply a blankness that denied the very possibility of life ever having existed here at all. The structure itself was nearing the state of the outer walls: the roof had sagged in the middle as if a giant had rested upon it on his travels; many windows had popped from their openings and shattered to the ground, or stood projecting from the walls, as if exploded from inside; Rick could see no signs of paint, only a dry crumbling rot in the timber which threatened to turn it all to powder at the slightest provocation.

He walked towards the closed front door, his heart still pumping excitement through his entire body, trying to remember the time he had fled this place several months before. All he could remember was someone lying in the front door opening. Whoever had been there then had now vanished, into or out of the house.

The front door tilted from its hinges with one hard shove and fell to the floor in a shower of dust. He knew where to go. He had no interest in the rest of the house, only the cellar. He started down the stone steps and flicked on the large torch he had brought with him.

The wall at the base of the steps was damp and slimy, the slow movement of thick water down its height seemed strangely out of place in the house, too lifelike. Rick froze for a second, half expecting a strangled scream to pierce the comfortable silence. None did, however, and he soon continued down the steps.

The basement was smaller than he remembered, hardly the size of a large bathroom. There were no signs of life at all: no mice, no insects, no spiders or their webs. It was as if life itself had fled the house, leaving it as a grim mausoleum to death, to nothingness. His torch flickered across the floor, twitched, moved back to what had caught his eye in the far corner of the basement.

A flash of white. He looked closer and saw the bones, scattered amongst the rags of an old coat. The skull sat on top, as if planted there purposefully, dried skin and hair still attached in paces. Rick squinted, feeling as if he was looking at the remnant though blurred glasses. He moved closer but the effect was the same; the eye sockets, jaw and nostril cavities seemed to blend and merge, blur at the edges as if there were two images overlapping.

Rick looked away, disconcerted, and before he could remember the truth of the Twin he saw the wall.

The wall of souls.

He noticed a face, the feature that drew him to the wall, and even from several feet away he vaguely recognised the image.

It was Damon. He could see the slight downcast set of his eyelids, the high cheekbones that may have suited a woman more. He looked closer, realising that he had been holding his breath, and blew dust from the surface of the face. It was set in stone, eternal, completely lifeless, the eyes shut and the forehead unfurrowed and peaceful.

He moved along the wall, seeing other faces along the way, one of which could have been the Mesmer as he was meant to be. His eyes, cast as they were in stone, were still somehow dark, pregnant with the potential for evil. Rick shivered, moved on, torch moving up and down, up and down, as he sought the final face.

Pen. He saw her. The eyes he had fallen in love with, closed but still showing the humour behind them in their set. Hair framing the face, long and flowing back into the wall, the stone cast impossibly thin in places so that separate hairs seemed to protrude from the masonry. Her mouth, the smile he had not seen since before she had died nearly nine years ago, and he had gone to her funeral, and buried her, and then started the long, painful process of mourning.

Rick reached out and touched her face for the last time, letting his fingers linger. Every millimetre he moved his fingers brought a fresh, sharp memory, rich in love and good humour. Every memory brought the tears closer, tears of fresh mourning that aged even as they fell to the stone floor of the cellar.

He stayed there for a long time, touching the cold, beautiful face of his dead girlfriend. Eventually he took his hand away, but he remained for several more hours, looking at her, until the batteries faded in his torch and it was time for him to go home.

THE END

ALSO FROM TANJEN

THE PARASITE

Neal L. Asher

Jack is the pilot of a cometary miner. On his final mission, the one which will make him rich, he encounters something in the hold of his ship, something which has been held in the ice of a comet for millennia.
Set in the future of military take overs, rising sea levels, and satellite industries, this is a story of high tech subterfuge and violence, which asks; what is it to be human? And what might the human race become?

ISBN 0952718316 — Price £5.99

"top quality SF from one of genre's hotshot new talents"
Dragon's Breath

"anyone who cares about the future of British literary SF should check it out"
SFX

EYELIDIAD

Rhys H. Hughes

Baron Darktree is a highwayman searching for gold he buried when he was younger. It's bad enough he has to put up with insults from his younger self (now a portrait he carries on his back), and that the map tattooed on his eyelid is no longer visible, but when he gets mistaken for Beer'or, the pagan god of golden beer, he begins to wonder how bad things can get.
Oh, much worse . . .

ISBN 0952718324 — Price £5.99

"Richly and hilariously imaginative, teeming with memorable images, and inimitably Welsh"
Ramsey Campbell

"the jaded fantasy reader will find much to enjoy here"
Flickers 'n' Frames

"imaginative slice of surrealist fantasy"
Samhain

RECLUSE

Derek M. Fox

A letter from a mysterious woman is all it takes to turn
Daniel Lees's world upside-down. He suspects his wife of
having an affair. He believes his children are in danger
from something that stalks the moors. He is haunted by a
past that will not leave him alone.
Finally he has to face up to what he really is and battle
against the nightmare that has threatened to destroy
everything he holds dear.

ISBN 1901530000 — Price £5.99

"*Recluse* is the chilling journey into the heart of a nightmare.
Reader beware – Derek M. Fox is set to be a new Master of
Fear."
Mark Chadbourn

"maintaining a cracking pace and an iron grip on the
reader's attention."
BBR Directory

PRISONERS OF LIMBO

David Ratcliffe

When the Carter family move to the new estate they hope it will mean the end of their troubles. Tommy Carter is never *out* of trouble, and Lucy Carter has a weakness for bad men. These hopes are soon dashed when they discover they are the only residents and the estate is half-finished. It soon becomes clear that somehow they have passed through a barrier of normality. In this world the dead are alive, the past is the present, and everything is in monochrome.
The problem is how to escape and return to the *real* world before it's too late.

ISBN 1901530043 — Price £5.99

"A dark, dirty tale — horror noir at its finest."
Night Dreams

SCATTERED REMAINS

Paul Pinn

A collection of short stories to celebrate the 750th anniversary of the Royal Bethlem Mental Hospital, the origin of the word bedlam. Each story is an examination of mental illness within the dark underbelly of human nature. Make sure you read this with the lights on.

ISBN 1901530051 — Price £6.99

"Soul-searing . . . totally bleak, remorseless and nihilistic."
Pam Creais, Dementia 13

"Black, claustrophobic, full of dirt and death . . . I like it."
Dave Logan, Grotesque Magazine

SCAREMONGERS

It will take a brave man or woman to read through this
collection in one sitting. Each story needs a deep breath
before starting and a moment of reflection on completion.
All your fears are here and if you remain umoved by the
end – you must already be *dead*.
Not for the fant-hearted.

A collection of short stories from some of the big names in
horror — Ramsey Campbell, Ray Bradbury,
Michael Marshall Smith, Simon Clark, Mark Chadbourn,
Stephen Laws, Poppy Z. Brite, Stephen Gallagher, Dennis
Etchison, Freda Warrington, Steve Harris, Ben Leech, Peter
Crowther, Nicholas Royle and many more.
All royalties donated to Animal Welfare Charities

ISBN 1901530078 — Price £6.99

DEMON

Derek M. Fox

Tibb's Cove ought to be a pleasant seaside town. But when
a Lancaster Bomber drops out of the night sky, and out of
the past, shooting up the place, it's anything but.
It's all to do with the war, and the game a group of local
boys played on the old airfield in 1954.
What dark secrets do the townspeople keep hidden? And
why is the aircrew back to terrorise the skies, exacting their
terrible revenge?
A cracking follow-up to *Recluse*.

ISBN 1901530019 — Price £5.99

coming in 1998

We Further praise for
Thank You, God, for These

"As a society, we value the company of animals, yet struggle
to find an appropriate way to deal with the loss of an animal
companion....The passages in this book will offer strength
and consolation for anyone dealing with grief over
the loss of a faithful companion."
—Douglas G. Aspros, D.V.M., Board of Directors,
National Board of Veterinary Medical Examiners

"For anyone who has ever loved and lost a pet,
this book is a 'must read.'"
—Edward C. Martin, Jr., Director, Hartsdale Canine
Cemetery, Inc., "America's First Pet Cemetery"

"This exquisitely beautiful book is absolutely sui generis.
It brings us closer into harmony with all God's creatures.
Francis of Assisi would have loved this sweet book.
He may even have inspired it."
—William O'Shaughnessy, Editorial Director,
Whitney Radio, Westchester, N.Y.

"I too have lost pets that meant a great deal to me and my
family. The moments spent grieving the loss of those pets
always seemed unfulfilled. Now after reading these prayers,
poems, and services, I am sure that those hard times, which
will undoubtedly come, will take on a new meaning and
fulfillment. Thank you for your inspired words!"
—Marc Muench, nature photographer